DRAGON
SKIN

KAREN FOXLEE was born in Mount Isa, Australia. She trained and worked as a nurse before studying for a degree in creative writing at the University of the Sunshine Coast. She is the author of five books, including *The Anatomy of Wings*, which won the Commonwealth Writer's Prize for Best First Book in the South East Asia and South Pacific region, and the Carnegie Medal-longlisted *Lenny's Book of Everything*, which is also published by Pushkin Children's Books.

KAREN FOXLEE

DRAGON SKIN

PUSHKIN CHILDREN'S

Pushkin Press
Somerset House, Strand
London wc2r 1la

The right of Karen Foxlee to be identified as the author of this Work has been
asserted by her in accordance with the Copyright, Designs & Patents Act 1988

Copyright © Karen Foxlee 2021

Dragon Skin was first published in Australia in 2021 by Allen & Unwin

First published by Pushkin Press in 2021

3 5 7 9 8 6 4

ISBN 13: 978-1-78269-299-7

Offset by Tetragon, London
Internal illustrations © Copyright Dale Newman 2021
Star illustrations © Midnight Grim/Creative Market
Printed and bound by Clays Ltd, Elcograf S.p.A.

www.pushkinpress.com

For my sister Ruth

ACT 1

ACT I

SHE DIDN'T WANT TO GO HOME AND THAT'S why she found it. If she'd gone home through the newly dark roads, washing her feet in streetlight pools, she would have found her mother in the kitchen making dinner looking scared. Matt would have come home and the screen door would have slammed hard and his tool bag would have crashed down on the kitchen bench. They would have flinched, her mother and her, waiting, but everything would have been normal.

She was the kind of girl who liked to dig with a stick in the dirt though. She liked to upturn things, searching for treasure: rocks, old bottles and silvery wine cask bladders, toothbrushes, coins, the carcasses of handbags. These strange things were swept up and snagged at the riverbend and left to dry once the water was gone. A wallet emptied out and brittle. Parts of a saddle. A belt buckle with the insignia of the silver mine.

She knew all the creek's white rock, all its blond grass and bleached trees. She knew the sun going down, the galahs screeching, rising and settling, rising and settling in the trees. She sat with her feet dipped in the waterhole and watched the night approach. The waterhole was a small deep pool of water that never dried up. It remained there even after the river flooded and then dried out to its normal self; a skin of stones and silt cracked into a million scales.

Mika always said, *Whatever you do Pip, take your feet out at night because that's when the bunyip comes out.*

She drew her feet out and sat in the dusk. Her stomach whined. Mika was a long time ago. Mika was months and months and months ago. The lights came on in the houses behind the trees. She felt the warm air against her wet legs. She waited for the part when the last ray of sun hit the creek stones, a brief moment when the whole riverbed shone and then was swallowed up by shadow. She promised herself she'd go home after that.

Only it was in that moment that she found it.

It didn't look like much at first, a scrap of something, fabric maybe, a snakeskin twisted around a stick perhaps, but that last wave of light caught it directly, shone it up bright, a burst of pinks and golds and greens, a small fire. Then was gone.

'Hey,' she said to herself and to the brand-new night. She was up, striding towards the spot just metres away, with her digging stick. 'Hey,' she said, softer, because she knew. She knew exactly what it was.

Later, she'd think about it over and over. When they were leaving and knew they'd never go back home again. When she'd grown that other skin. She knew what it was before she stood up. Even before she saw it shining there. She'd *always* known it.

SHE KEPT ITS SMALL HUSK OF A BODY CLOSE
to her chest as she walked home through the streets.
She made a cradle with her T-shirt and nursed it there.
It was the size of a small kitten, hairless, a little lump
for its belly and legs curled beneath. There was a tangle
of something on its back, like fishing net. It was half-
dead. Almost dead. It made a sound as she nursed it, a
dry leaf sound, a dying sound. 'It'll be okay, Little Fella,'
she said to it. 'It'll be okay.'

Her house was three streets from the creek and
her feet could have walked her there by themselves.
All the houses were the same, each and every one.
Mining company houses with pale corrugated skins,

six cement stumps and one small patio. Each house she passed, the outdoor air conditioners shuddered and hummed to themselves. Some evenings that's all you could hear; air conditioners thrumming and out on the highway the road trains coming in from the desert sounding their horns.

She passed the Lees' house, keeping her head down and the thing wrapped up in her shirt. Mrs Lee, watering her buffalo grass in the dark, saw her though.

'What are you doing out so late again, Pip?'

'Nothing,' said Pip.

Mrs Lee raised the hose and sprayed water after Pip's feet. 'Hope you're not stealing Mrs Watson's pawpaws again?' she called, laughing. Pip was already running, turning the corner to home.

Pip wanted to stop, to look again at its dark withered shape, but she didn't. When she'd glanced at it beneath the first streetlight home, her heart had swelled and it had been a sorrowful rushing inflation. She needed to help it soon or it would die.

'It'll be okay Little Fella,' she whispered, opening the metal front gate as quietly as she could. She needed a plan yet a plan evaded her. There was no plan for someone home late carrying a nearly dead dragon.

*

'Pippa,' shouted her mother. 'Don't you try to sneak past me!'

She must have heard Pip's footsteps in the hallway, even though Pip had tiptoed. Pip ran the last steps to her room and pulled a hoodie from a drawer and made a little nest for the creature on a shelf in her wardrobe.

'Pippa!' This time it was even louder.

'I'm coming,' said Pip. One last glance at the thing lying curled there. 'Ouch,' she said because her heart had done that thing again. That big thing. An aching swell like a kicked toe grown fat. Could kids have heart attacks the way old people did? She shut the wardrobe as her mother appeared at her bedroom door.

'Ouch?' said her mum, looking at Pip standing there holding her heart. 'What? Are you hurt?'

'No,' said Pip.

'Where've you been?' Softer, her eyes moving to Pip's dirty legs, the scratches over her shins, and then up to her tear-streaked face. 'Creek again? Seriously, Pip. You know we've talked about this.'

'Sorry,' said Pip.

'It's a school night.'

'I know, but school is nearly finished.'

'It's so late. It's dark for god's sake. You're ten.'

'I was just sitting there,' said Pip. 'I forgot time.'

That wasn't true. She never forgot time. She knew every single moment of time at the creek at dusk. The shadowy stripes of the silver box trees falling down into the lap of stones. The sun dipping down to wink behind the bent branch of a ghost gum, the number of rises and falls it took for the galahs to go to sleep.

'I promise,' Pip said, not even sure what she was promising.

'He's not coming back,' said her mum. 'He is *not* coming back.'

'I know that,' Pip whispered.

Pip took the embrace her mother offered; a sweaty, gym pants, gardening-smell hug. She must have been trying to save her dying roses again. The angry moment had passed. Her mother could never stay angry for long.

'It'll be all right,' said her mother. 'It's okay to be sad. Don't hang out there at night. Okay? Hanging out in the dark doesn't change anything. Quickly, shower. I've made spaghetti.'

'Okay,' said Pip.

At the dining room table, Pip twirled her spaghetti.

'It was hot,' said her mum, sitting opposite, 'about an hour ago.'

'I'm not complaining,' said Pip.

She was wondering if the dragon was still alive in the little hoodie nest. It had been after the world's fastest shower. She'd peeked into the wardrobe and seen its little belly rising and falling, heard its ever so small rasping breath. The sorrowful swelling in her chest almost lifted her off the ground. She was wondering how to save a dragon.

Stay calm Pip, Mika said quietly in her head. *Keep your nerve. Eat your spaghetti and think. What do you need to save a dragon?*

Relief made her sink back into her chair. She was

always so glad when he spoke to her. Just when she thought he'd gone for good, there he was.

Remember that time we saved Ursa? Mika said. *Remember?*

Kittens are different to dragons, she silently answered him.

'Eat up,' said Mum. 'Look you're hardly even touching your dinner and it's so late and Matt will be home soon if you don't hurry and what will he say if he sees you still sitting here eating dinner and not in bed?'

It was a rhetorical question. Pip needn't have answered. Matt liked Pip in her room with the light off and the door closed so he could have her mum all to himself. He didn't like any competition. Competition made him angry.

'He'll go off his brain.'

That was the wrong answer. There was the glimmer of tears in her mum's eyes.

'Eat up, okay?' she said.

Pip, you are going to need medical supplies and food, Mika said. *Sugary food. Sugar helps sick things.*

'I'm going as fast as I can,' Pip said to her mother. 'I mean, spaghetti is the least fast-eating food there is.'

Her mother laughed.

'God, what am I going to do with you?' she said.

'Don't know.' Pip smiled back, mouth full of spaghetti. But she was thinking about the dragon in her wardrobe.

THE THING WITH DRAGONS WAS THAT NO ONE expected to find one. No one in the world would be ready for such a thing. There was no section in the library between Pet Care and Gardening called Dragon Care. Pip looked at her mother who was looking at her phone. Pip would have told her if it was in the before time. She would have told her and her mother would have listened the way she used to listen. Not like now, like she could only half-hear. Like she had a song in her head or a puzzle she was trying to solve.

She would have stopped whatever she was doing and come to help.

Her mother smiled a half-smile as she scrolled.

One-minute quiz what's your body type five fail-safe recipes seven-day meal prep for weight loss see the great barrier reef five best workouts to blast belly fat does he really love you online oracle fifty-day declutter your life challenge summer dresses to suit your body shape common problems with roses, why are my roses dying?

'I better have a shower,' her mother said, still staring into the screen. 'You get ready for bed.'

Pip searched through the medicine drawer in the kitchen when she heard the shower turn on. The drawer contained sting cream and bandaids and Ichthammol, which her mother used for drawing out rose thorns. Panadol, asthma puffers and an eye-dropper, which Pip put in her dressing-gown pocket. Mika and her had used that eye-dropper for a baby bird they'd found on the way home from school. They'd kept it in an empty margarine carton and dropped water into its mouth until Pip's mum had taken it to the vet.

See, there was the bird too, remember that? We've got a good track record at saving things.

She found a plastic syringe. A plastic syringe would be perfect! Her grandmother was a wildlife carer in

Townsville; she'd seen her use a syringe with a baby possum.

Herbal sleeping tablets, Deep Heat gel, anti-fungal toe cream. Her fingers flicked through the drawer. She took the bandaids. A pair of scissors. Two cups of water, a spoon and the sugar pot. Eye-dropper and syringe aside, none of it really seemed like the type of stuff that could save a dragon.

When her supplies were safely in the top drawer of her bedside table, she stood at her door until the shower stopped.

'Good night.'

'Night.' Her mum kissed Pip on the forehead. 'You okay?'

'Yes,' said Pip, even though she had a dragon to save.

In her bedroom with the night light on and her door closed, she scooped the little thing out of the wardrobe in its hoodie nest. She sat with it in her lap, curled, the way a caterpillar curls itself when something wants to eat it. Its head was much bigger than its body and that head was nestled down inside the circle its body made. Its long tail looped around it. It didn't have spikes, the way dragons in stories had spikes, but on its back and tail there were small tufts of papery stuff. It had the nubs of two little horns upon its nose. She resisted the urge to touch them even though the urge was strong. It was definitely a baby dragon. Not a lizard. Not a baby croc.

'I'm not imagining you,' she whispered to it.

It had three claws on each foot, caked in river dust, and its body was coated all over too, as though it had laid there for a long time.

'I'm not imagining you, am I?'

It was thin. Its rib cage showed with each tiny breath. Its wings were tangled. At least she thought they were wings: they were dark, delicate, completely in tatters, the way old black garbage bags looked at the dump, stuck to barbed wire fences. They were torn.

She would have to fix those rips but first she'd have to stop it from dying.

She heard her mother's footsteps in the hall and held her breath.

'Love you,' her mother said, then, 'remember to turn out your night-light too.'

Remember to disappear. Remember to stay quiet. Remember to not exist.

'I will,' said Pip. 'Love you.'

She spooned sugar into a cup and mixed in water.

She sucked up the liquid with a syringe and tentatively placed her finger on the little dragon's mouth, moved it gently, carefully, trying to find a place to insert the tip. It didn't move, just took its tiny rasping breaths. Small, sharp teeth by the glow of her night-light and right at the back, a very small gap. She inserted the syringe tip and squirted slowly.

It dribbled out.

She tried again.

The little thing made a gurgling noise.

'It's okay, Little Fella,' she whispered. 'You have to swallow.'

She swapped to the eye-dropper. She placed her fingers against the snout, prised gently, opening the tiny mouth filled with needle-sharp teeth and a dry thing that could only be its tongue. She squeezed the bulb of the eye-dropper gently and let a single drop of sugary liquid fall into the mouth.

'Come on, Little Fella.' Its tiny body convulsed in response to the drop and she saw the rippling of its throat as it swallowed.

She arranged her equipment on her bedside table quickly. Cup of sugary water. Eye-dropper. Tissues for mopping up excess dribble. She kept one hand on mouth-opening duty and one hand for eye-dropper duty. She let the dragon rest after each three drops. Three drops was all it seemed to manage before that rippling swallow weakened and the liquid pooled from the side of its little mouth.

The light from the television in her mother's room bled under her door. Green, then blue, then white. Her mum would be staring into that light. Rhinestone caftans, knives that never go blunt, steam mops, ab-trainers. The complete crystal healing set. Bach flower oils, the robo-vacuum, holiday clubs. Her mum would gaze into that glow like a princess into a pond, wishing and wishing.

In the pauses between swallows, Pip touched the dragon's scales with her fingertips. They felt strange but, even stranger, not unfamiliar. She had never touched a dragon before, she was one hundred per cent certain, yet she felt like she had. There was no explaining that. And she was almost certain, suddenly, that Little Fella was a boy. She had no knowledge of how to confirm this, just knew.

'You're going to be all right,' she told him, lying there curled in her lap. 'Little Fella, that's your name.'

Little Fella.

She whispered it, again and again. In the darkened room she fed him and whispered to him without stopping for what seemed like hours. Three drops. Rest. Three drops. Rest. Three drops. Rest.

When she heard the screen door slam open and Matt's tool bag crash down onto the kitchen bench, those sounds barely registered. Even the sound of her mother's quick, soft footsteps, ready to placate him, seemed to come from a faraway place.

PIP WOKE TO DAWN LIGHT AND THE EYE-dropper still in her hand. The dragon had vomited in the bed beside her. It was a dark spray over the hoodie and part of the pillow. The outside of the dragon might have been dry and shrivelled but the inside of him smelled wild; grassy, sky-filled and tart as grapefruit.

He was also dead.

She'd come up from her dreams like a deep-sea diver and there he was, not breathing.

'Please,' she whispered, searching for the rise and fall of his chest.

There was nothing.

She pulled at her hair and one single high-pitched squeal escaped from her. There was a lament, hurricane-sized, just waiting to burst from her lungs. She squeezed her hands into fists and banged against her own chest and opened her mouth, soundless, because she was useless at saving things, because he shouldn't have died, because sugary water was probably the wrong thing and she'd killed him. Because this was her one and only chance to save a dragon and he had depended on her.

The dragon suddenly took one long shuddering breath, coughed weakly, blew dark vomit from his nostrils.

Pip gasped.

Little Fella took another shuddering breath, shifted, curled himself tighter, the first time he'd moved. Pip gasped again. He shuddered again, breathed more black vomit from his nostrils. They gasped and breathed at each other until Pip was laughing through her tears.

'That was seriously bad,' she whispered to him, to herself. 'Seriously bad. You can't die.'

She scooped him up in the hoodie and placed him in her wardrobe again. She looked at the vomit on her pillow, decided it was a problem. She removed the pillowcase and quickly thrust it under her bed, pulled her sheet up over the remaining flecks across the top of the bed. She dressed in her school uniform even though she knew she wouldn't be going to school.

In the bathroom she gauged the sounds of the house. It was quiet apart from the sound of the frying pan. That would be her mother cooking breakfast for Matt. There were no voices. She stared at her reflection: brown hair, brown eyes, freckles. A large mole on her right cheek. She didn't look like someone who was saving a dragon.

She listened for Mika's voice in her head. It didn't arrive. She hated that emptiness. He never came much in the mornings, she knew, but she'd thought, considering the circumstances, that he might.

So, he nearly died, she told Mika as she tied her hair into a rough ponytail. *He didn't, so that's good news. Obviously, I can't go to school.*

She waited several seconds. Nothing. She knew she was only stalling anyway. She went down the hall into the dining room.

'Hi Matt,' she said.

'Morning,' he said, and didn't look up from his phone.

She wondered, if he did look up, would he see it on her, all that finding a dragon and nearly losing it? All that dragon-saving? She hoped he wouldn't look up.

He was dangerous. Dangerous like water. He could seem calm and glassy on top but underneath he was all dark silt and weed.

He was big too, probably as big as a bear if a bear were in their kitchen standing on its hind legs. Sometimes as ferocious. Now he was sitting drinking his coffee and scrolling through Facebook stealing all the oxygen. Her mother and her had to survive on small sips of air.

'I was nearly coming to wake you,' her mum said quietly. 'You're going to be late.'

'I was out to it,' said Pip.

Pip made Weet-Bix. Weet-Bix might be good for Little Fella. Weet-Bix made kids strong. Maybe it would be the same for a dragon.

In the dining room she sat opposite Matt.

He asked her if she had done her homework. He didn't look up from the phone for the question.

'There's no homework,' she said. 'It's the last week of term.'

He laughed at that, still scrolling. A harsh, scornful laugh, as though that was the most ridiculous thing he'd ever heard. Like she'd said, *We're never having homework again. Homework is history. Homework no longer exists.*

She never knew what was going to annoy him. She wished, very quickly, several times, for him not to be annoyed that this was the last week of term and that there was no homework.

What if she said, *I found a dragon. I found him in the creek when the sun was falling down. I found him and he needs to be saved and I've been up all night saving him. I thought he was dead but he breathed again.* What if she said that?

He didn't continue the conversation, kept scrolling. Pip felt she'd escaped something momentarily, then checked herself just as fast.

That's how it was.

He was dangerous like the hairpin bends in a road.

You didn't really know what was coming the other way.

'How about I drive you this morning?' said Mum, putting down the plate in front of Matt. It was perfect. The toast, the eggs, the bacon. Yet Pip watched his eyes searching for something to fault. He didn't say thank you. It was on Pip's tongue, to say thank you for him.

'I'm right to ride,' said Pip. Matt didn't like her mum driving the four-wheel drive.

'Let her ride,' said Matt. 'It's good for her.'

Because he was in charge of everything. What was good for them, or what wasn't.

You're going to need arrowroot biscuits, said Mika abruptly in her head. It gave her such a fright she jumped in her chair. *Remember the story I told you about the baby on the station, a long way from a hospital, that was sick and fading fast then they mushed up arrowroot biscuit and—*

'Well, you better eat up quick,' said her mum. 'It's late, you know.'

'Good bacon,' said Matt. Pip glanced up and into the kitchen and saw her mum's shoulders relax.

That's how quickly it could change. There was suddenly air again, like a vent had been opened.

Pip ate her Weet-Bix as quickly and quietly as she could and then went back to the kitchen to take her lunch box.

'What are you looking for, Pippa?' asked her mum when she was down in the bottom shelves of the pantry again.

'Muesli bars,' said Pip, even though she wasn't. She was searching for arrowroot biscuits.

'I already packed you one,' said Mum.

'Maybe some arrowroots,' said Pip. 'I just really feel like some.'

'Hurry up,' whispered Mum, going past her to take coffee to Matt. She obviously didn't want anything to ruin Matt's brand-new shiny good mood. Pip grabbed the entire packet when her mother was out of the kitchen and thrust it into her schoolbag.

School, she thought. *One hundred per cent impossible.*

In her room she bundled up Little Fella in the hoodie. He had vomited again and that was a bad sign. Maybe the sugar was one hundred per cent a bad idea.

Maybe dragons were sugar intolerant. He wasn't curled tight anymore, he was limper. He looked smaller and more dried out again. Flattened-toad dry. But he was still breathing.

Into her schoolbag on top of the arrowroot biscuits went the dropper and the syringe. The cup, a water bottle. She placed Little Fella, wrapped in the hoodie nest, on top, staring until she saw the tiny rise and fall of his chest, rechecking again, in case her eyes were playing tricks on her. Her heart ached like an old broken bone in the cold.

She wondered again if she should tell her mother. Even while her mother kissed her and Pip was being careful not to look into her eyes in case her mother saw the lie, she was wondering it.

She knew she couldn't.

If she told her mum, then her mum would tell Matt and Matt owned everything. Her mother had to tell him everything because he was the king of knowing everything.

He'd say, one hundred per cent, they'd have to put it out of its misery.

S HE DIDN'T GO DOWN THE LONG, STRAIGHT
road that ran beside the creek to school. She turned
left onto the road that crossed the creek instead. There
was a still heat, no wind, like the inside of an oven just
turned on. That heat would increase as the sun rose.
That heat baked the skin of the dry creek. It cooked
the bitumen and cracked it open like the top of a pie.
It burned the swings in the park so that you couldn't
touch them and sucked all the colour from everything:
out of grass, out of leaves, out of clothes left on the
line. She rode as fast as she could.

She hoped that leaving later than normal would
help her avoid other school kids. Angus Barton or

Audrey Coles or Lucy and Emily Cartwright, the twins, at the bottom of Buna Street, who'd always call out, and pedal behind her quickly, singing out, *Pippa, Pippa, wait for us.*

She wasn't lucky though. There on the other side of the crossing was Archie Morgan. She swore under her breath. He was on his BMX and he was going to stop her for sure. Archie lived on the other side of the creek and she should have remembered that.

He stopped in the middle of the crossing; a road built across the dry river that disappeared completely when it flooded. He was smiling, his streak of dyed orange hair glowing in the morning sun.

'Hi,' she said.

'Hi,' he said. 'You're going the wrong way.'

Pip shrugged, glanced at the sky.

Archie Morgan, suddenly keeper of the bridge and that side of town, with the hills she needed and the rocks and the caves, seemed like he was going to let her pass. She hoped Little Fella wasn't suffocating in her backpack.

'You wagging?' he asked. 'You're going to get in real big trouble, Pip.'

Sometimes Archie had hung out with Mika and her. Some afternoons down the creek, if he'd spotted them there at the Junkyard on the swing, he'd come to sit on a rock and talk with them. He'd never made jokes about Pip and Mika, the way other kids did. Love and marriage and a baby carriage. That kind of stuff.

'I'm not wagging,' she said. 'I've just got to drop something somewhere.'

'Drop *something*?' he said. *'Somewhere?'*

'Yeah.'

'Okay,' he said, long and slow.

'I'm *not* wagging,' she said again and started to ride.

He laughed and started to ride too, in the opposite direction, not even looking back over his shoulder.

'Will you tell?' she called after him but he didn't answer.

He probably won't, she thought as she rode furiously, *he isn't that kind of kid*. But she couldn't know for sure.

The other side of the creek was an industrial estate:

a tyre place, a truck mechanic, a vet surgery, the old rollerskating rink with its padlocked fence and its once colourful sign covered in graffiti. ROLLER-FUN. Horse paddocks with horses crowded in any shade they could find, and then the hills.

There were other faded suburbs with bleached gardens behind the hills and the old cemetery, with its quartz rock grave markers and in a small slice of green, the lawn cemetery, where the sprinklers whirred constantly, trying to defy the desert sun. Yet it was the hills she needed. *Their* hill.

Mika and her had practically lived at the hill on weekends but they didn't know about the cave in the beginning. They'd explored for days before they found it, each time dropping her bike down into the gully beside the road and clambering up through the spinifex and rocky spines.

Mika touched those rocks. He ran his fingers over them. He crouched down and spent time examining them. He said serious things like, 'When these rocks were formed this would have all been the sea,' or, 'This rock is older even than the dinosaurs.'

Pip didn't know where he got his information from, but he said these things with such conviction that she wanted to believe him. She was only nine then and she'd never met another kid her age that spoke like that. It made her laugh nervously yet feel excited, like standing near him made the world feel bigger. She got butterflies each morning when she saw him waiting for her at the end of the street.

Their hill had three distinct sides, which led Mika to hypothesise that it was the remains of an ancient pyramid built by aliens. The rocky spines had once been its walls. She'd squinted against the sun, hand over her brow, and said, 'Seriously?'

She knew from the welcome to country that the land belonged to the Kalkatungu people and they'd been living there since forever and she was pretty sure they would have noticed a whole heap of aliens building a pyramid.

But nothing, she'd learn, made Mika's stories flourish more than a sceptic. Soon he could tell her which planet they'd come from, what system of government they had, even what clothes they wore. The smile on his face grew with each fact. He stood there describing it all, his pale face burning in the sun. Mika believed in almost everything, and aliens were his favourite.

'This was ages ago,' he said. 'Like forever ago. And they were only here for a really short time.'

'Just to build a pyramid in the middle of nowhere,' said Pip, smiling back at him before picking her way further up the hill through the red rock and yellow grass.

She stood there now on the side of the road, remembering, the dragon in her backpack. She wheeled her bike off the road and dumped it in the gully so it wouldn't be seen, then clambered up the other side and began to climb. *Their* hill. There were countless other red rock hills patched with spinifex and spiny outcrops of rocks but this was *their* hill and she hadn't been back since he'd gone away.

The cave wasn't a deep cave, more a rock overhang. It was completely hidden from view and that's why they hadn't found it for a long time. The desert side of the hill was all rock face and ledges and small slanting segments of spinifex and stacked shale. They'd climbed backwards and then dropped from rocks onto a ledge just to see what was there and found it waiting.

It was tricky, that dropping down bit.

It took courage.

She'd forgotten that because together they'd grown used to being brave.

Inside the cave the floor was packed hard and smooth. It was cool inside and now, she slid her bum backwards into that space. The morning shimmered outside the cave as she unzipped her bag, ignoring her own thirst, and took out the hoodie.

Her hands shook.

Little Fella took tiny rasping breaths.

He looked terrible.

'It'll be okay, Little Fella,' she promised, as she went to work crushing up arrowroot biscuit and mixing it with water.

At first when she fed him, she wished, over and over, for him not to die. It wasn't normal wishing. Not Christmas present wishing or birthday wishing, it was big wishing, sky-sized, *I'll trade you something huge* wishing, *I'll never think another bad thought about Matt again* wishing. 'Don't die, don't die, don't die,' she whispered, like there might be some power in saying those words.

She mushed the arrowroot and prised open his tiny mouth and dropped a single pearl of the liquid onto his tongue. He wouldn't swallow. He was almost lifeless apart from the tiny rise and fall of his chest, the tremor of his heartbeat.

'Please don't die,' she whispered.

Saving Ursa had been straightforward. All that kitten had needed was warmth and milk. Mika's gran, Mrs Jarvinen, had told them she was going to have to call the pound although, in the end, she'd relented. She'd driven them in her sunbird with its clunking gears all the way to Kmart Plaza so they could buy special kitten food.

Food and Warmth and Love.

Mika said he'd always wished for a kitten.

Wishes like that were tiny in comparison to how much she wished in the cave for the dragon to not die.

A drop in the ocean of wishing for the dragon to survive.

She stroked beneath his chin and he responded to that, the tiniest of swallows.

'That's it, Little Fella.'

Another drop of mushed arrowroot mixed with water.

Don't die, don't die, don't die.

She could hear his breathing now. Sick breathing. Rattly. Maybe all she was doing was drowning him. It was a terrible thing to find a dragon and not know how to save it.

Another tiny swallow.

Don't die, don't die, don't die.

She stroked his chin and inserted another drop.

Don't die, don't die, don't die.

Those words lost their shape after a while. They melted into something else, a kind of song. A low lilting song. A kind of keening.

What are you doing? she asked herself.

She kept on singing.

That's it, said Mika. *Don't stop.*

She was glad he was back again but she couldn't have stopped it if she wanted to.

Because it wasn't even just singing, it was crying too. She was singing a mournful song over Little Fella and she was crying tears as well. That sorrowful rushing inflation in her heart turned to tears up there in the hill's mouth, it filled up her eyes and there were cool tears sliding down her cheeks, dripping one by one onto the tiny half-dead dragon.

Those tears and strange words were like snot from a nose. A tap turned on. She cried and sang and the tears dripped onto the little thing in her lap, onto his dusty dark scales, onto the eye-dropper in her hand, onto the arrowroot biscuit mush. She was a fount of tears. It didn't seem possible that she could have so many inside her.

Maybe it's magic, she thought as she cried, as the tears dripped onto her hands, into the gruel, onto the dry black scales. Since finding the dragon she hadn't once thought of magic but now, when she did, she felt breathless and like she might need the toilet. Her bowels gurgled suddenly. She clutched her belly.

How was she going to know what to do with magic?

She was just a kid from Chimbu Street.

She knew nothing.

Nothing at all about magic.

And she was pretty sure magic wasn't meant to be arrowroot biscuit mushed up in water or dragon vomit in your bed. Not tears on her dirty face or the sorrowful taste of song, that she couldn't know but somehow knew, sliding off her tongue.

Surely it wasn't.

Stay calm, Pip, said Mika in her head.

MIKA BELIEVED IN MAGIC. ONE HUNDRED per cent without a doubt. She learned that fast when he arrived. He knew the Dewey decimal 130s like the back of his hand and they went to the town library often to sit in front of them. The 130s were bottom shelf; Occult and Paranormal. He ran his fingertips along those spines muttering to himself. 'This is nowhere near as good as the Oxley Library, Pip.'

Spells to summon storms. Spells to summon back spirits from the afterlife. Spectral gates to other worlds. Other worlds themselves. Other worlds with werewolves. Definitely werewolves.

He scared himself sick with his belief in werewolves.

He believed in the supernatural. Ghosts. Ectoplasm. Poltergeists. Spirit orbs. He said everyone has a doppelganger. Everyone. 'Somewhere in the world Pip, there's another you. There's another me. And in another universe, we're there as well, doing something else.'

She always shook her head at that.

'There's only one me, and only one you,' she'd argue back although she had as little proof as him.

Portals. Rifts. Wormholes that allowed interstellar travel.

He believed in intelligent life in outer space.

Typical Mika question: 'If a spaceship landed at Gallipoli Park, Pip, middle of the night, and asked us to come on board and see the universe, only catch, we could never come back, what would you do?'

Pip hated questions like that. In the beginning they shocked her. Made her feel physically unwell because her brain didn't work like that.

She was black and white. Vegemite or Marmite.

Chocolate or vanilla. Chewing gum or Hubba Bubba. Nothing bigger. Not: Never see your mother again versus see the universe.

Mika lived with his great-grandmother and he'd been sent there from the city. He'd arrived at the end of Grade Three, at the classroom door with a green backpack that was way too big for him, smiling his secretive Mika smile as though he found the whole situation amusing.

He'd been sent on a train. Two whole nights and a day alone, he told the class on that first day when the teacher asked where he'd come from. 'It's called *The Inlander*,' he said, 'but first I went on *The Spirit of Queensland*. I saw some gum trees at night that shone like gold in the moonlight.' That shut everyone up. 'I only had twenty bucks for the whole trip so every time I got a cheese toastie, I had to save half of it for later. It was like *Survivor* on a train. I nearly had to drink the water that had a sign above it that said "DO NOT DRINK THIS WATER", but then this nice lady gave me money for a bottle of water. I was fully dehydrated.'

He never really answered the question of where he'd come from, though the entire Grade Three class was, by that stage, enthralled.

'Something's different here, Pip,' he'd say at the waterhole, at the side of the highway, at the top of Gallipoli Park. 'Can you feel it? Like there's a portal nearby.'

'What even is a portal?' she'd say, watching him. He was skinny, although Mrs Jarvinen had put some weight on him since he arrived. His white-blonde hair flopped down over his eyes. His nails were permanently dirty because he liked to dig for things too.

'So, you can't feel it?'

'Just feels like hot air,' Pip would answer.

The creek *did* have places that felt different, though. Where the air changed. Where it felt heavier or lighter or strangely still, expectant, like something was about to happen. She didn't want to give away too much to him back then. In the beginning.

'I wish I had a sonic screwdriver,' he'd say, kind of sadly, like it actually was a real thing. He'd hold the invisible wished-for sonic screwdriver in his hand and point it to the sky. 'I could scan for the types of life forms here. Or close by, in another realm. Maybe burn a hole into another realm.'

'What's wrong with this realm?' she'd say. To annoy him more than anything. There was *everything* wrong with this realm. Mika had arrived two weeks after Matt had moved into her house. Two weeks of an entire strange new realm.

As the memory faded, the singing dried out on her tongue. The tears dried on her cheeks. The sun rose, white-hot, burning momentarily into the cave then passing, rising, rising. The shade slid across the cave floor, covering Pip and the dragon like a blanket and velvet geckos, hidden from view, ticked softly in the new shadows. She wondered what would be happening at school. Maybe they were doing the Christmas card activity that had been promised yesterday.

'We're going to make some pretty cool cards for our mums and dads,' Mr T had announced.

'Have you got a dad, Pip?' Laura Denning, who sat in front of her, had turned to whisper.

It was said in a sickly-sweet voice. Pink ribbons braided through her hair.

Pip had flipped her the bird.

'Pippa, you know we don't do things like that here,' said Mr T.

She hoped they were doing that activity right now. They'd be colouring in while she was on a hill, saving a dragon. She smiled at that.

She had stopped feeding him because he'd grown tired. His swallow, which had grown stronger, had weakened. Pip thought she could see behind those leathery closed eyelids, the eyeballs moving, the way she'd see Matt's moving when he was passed out on the sofa on a Saturday afternoon. Was it a good sign? *He's come from nearly dead to dreaming*, she thought. *One day he'll open his eyes.* The colour would be blue or green, she couldn't decide, though definitely not red like a dragon in a picture book. She was so glad that her weird crying had stopped. That crying was the strangest thing. That crying was deep like an ocean that no one could ever touch the bottom of.

She watched his breathing. His breathing was

definitely settled. There weren't so many pauses and then the jagged shuddering catch-up gasps. The little heartbeat had slowed too, beneath that bony rib cage.

'Where have you come from? Did you fall from the sky?' she asked.

'Maybe . . .' she started. 'Maybe your . . . mother dropped you?'

'By accident,' she added quickly.

The sun climbed. She'd be in trouble. That was at the back of her mind. The school would have rung her mother to report her absence. It would be Mrs Green from the office and she'd say, *Hi there, just wanting to check that Pippa is with you, Melissa?* Her mother would sigh, *No, no she's not with me.* After all, it wasn't like she hadn't done it before. Her mother would know she was at the creek, or somewhere hidden in the hills but it still wouldn't stop her worrying and that hurt Pip.

Okay, well I'm really sorry Mrs Green, I'll go and look for her, okay?

She was probably walking around right now looking for Pip. It would be Monumental-End-of-the-Earth-Trouble.

Then Little Fella coughed. It was a big cough for something so small. He opened his mouth wide and she saw for a few seconds deep inside two rows of razor teeth, one behind the other, the dryness of his dark tongue. A gob of spit came hurtling out and hit the ground and sizzled. He didn't wake and he looked more comfortable for having that out. He uncurled unexpectedly and extended his four feet the way a kitten might stretch, then curled himself tight again. He made a rattly noise like a tiny maraca. All the trouble with her mum aside, Pip knew she'd done the right thing.

Told you arrowroots would work, said Mika.

The sun reached its zenith and started its slow trek down. The cave grew even darker and cooler. She tenderly placed Little Fella in his hoodie nest onto the dirt and went outside to pee. She climbed out of the cave into the sun and down and around a spine of rocks, all of them flat and red, slammed into each other by some cataclysmic force eons ago. She pulled down her school shorts and squatted, watched the trail of wee forge a river through the red dirt.

Little Fella was better. She knew it inside her. Or getting better. And with that knowledge came sudden exhaustion. She went back into the cave and lay down on the dirt beside him.

I wonder how big it will get? asked Mika inside her.

'It's a he,' said Pip.

I wonder how big he'll get?

'Big,' said Pip. 'I won't see him when he's big though.'

How do you know?

'I dunno. Just a feeling.'

She closed her eyes. She could have sworn it was for a second, yet when she opened them again the sun was low and the hummock grass glowed golden by its setting. 'Come on Little Fella,' she said and placed him carefully, hoodie and all, down inside her backpack. All the way back to her bike she could feel the new weight of him. She pedalled slowly, coasting down the hill, drifting across the intersections towards the crossing to where her mother was standing, waiting.

They walked in silence at first, then: 'Do you think I'm a fool?'

'No,' said Pip.

'Do you think I'm a fool?' her mother asked again.

'No,' said Pip, 'really, I don't. I'm sorry.'

'Do you think I want to walk around all day looking for you?'

'No.'

'Do you think that's fun for me?'

Pip's mum had sold her car to help pay off Matt's four-wheel drive, except he hardly ever let her drive it.

'I'm sorry.'

'You aren't sorry,' said her mother. 'You say sorry and then you keep doing the thing again. This running away. This not going to school. Ever since . . .'

'Mika,' said Pip. No one could say his name.

But she *was* sorry for everything. Sorry for running away. Sorry for hating school. Sorry for Mika. Sorry for Mika's mum. Sorry for her own mum, who kept trying to be better, trying to exercise and trying to be a goddess in six easy steps while always wishing she were someone else. And sorry for Matt who had a heart made out of stone. Sorry for all of them. Sorry for their house, which was exactly the same as all the others, yet somehow looked darker. Sorry for the dragon in her backpack who'd lost his own mum and ended up in her care.

They walked past Mrs Lee, watering her buffalo grass. She didn't say anything to them. Simply watched.

At home, her mother told her to go to her room but Pip knew it wasn't over. Her mother was too calm. There would be more crying and maybe some yelling. Her mother would come back again with a catalogue of everything Pip had ever done wrong. Running away, not doing homework, not eating like a normal child, being too secretive, being too lonely, being too impulsive, never being sorry, not accepting consequences, constantly lying. It was all going to come down that hall in a great flood.

She reached into the backpack to take out Little Fella. Her eyes were on the door, waiting for her mother, when she felt a sudden sharp pain, like a knitting needle had been jammed into her left palm.

'Hey!' She ripped back her hand.

She looked into the backpack and expected to see Little Fella staring back up at her. He was still sleeping.

She inspected her bleeding hand. It wasn't the teeth that got her. Those tiny sharp teeth would have ripped her hand apart. This was a deep hole in her palm, filling up like a well with blood. A claw mark.

She took an old handkerchief from her wardrobe drawer and clenched it in her palm to stop the bleeding. She put her hands into the bag again, slowly. She touched Little Fella and he didn't move, so she dug her fingers beneath the hoodie and scooped him up. He made the small, contented maraca sound. Out of the bag and up and into the wardrobe in time for her mother's footsteps.

'You never used to be like this,' said her mother, standing at the door, her arms crossed. 'I mean, I know things have been tough—'

'You used to be different too,' Pip interrupted, pressing the handkerchief into her palm. She stared right into her mother's eyes until her mother glanced away.

'I think I need to take you to a psychologist or something, find some help for you,' her mother said. 'It's the lying that bothers me.'

'I'm really sorry,' said Pip.

But they were all just words patched over the great surface of things. Her mother lied all the time. She lied to herself. She lied to Pip that everything was going to be okay. She lied that everything was going to get better. She lied when she said she was leaving Matt. They never left.

Pip's hand was aching. A deep rose thorn ache. It felt wet and sticky where it was bleeding into the handkerchief.

'Do you want me to make the dinner, Mum?'

'There's no dinner,' said her mum. 'Get in the bath.'

HER MOTHER COULD NEVER STAY ANGRY for long, though. When Pip climbed into bed, she appeared with eggs and toast and a bandaid.

'How'd you do it?' her mum asked.

'Spinifex,' Pip lied. A pause while her mother watched her eyes. 'I tripped and fell into a whole patch of it.'

A bandaid wasn't going to work, so after Pip had finished eating her mum left and returned with a pad and bandage.

'That's deep,' her mother said, dressing the wound, then tucking the blanket up around her chin. Outside the night was singing, cicadas humming themselves loose from their skins and above, Pip knew, the stars would be blazing. *Parents like you better when you're injured,* she thought. *It's a fact.*

'I know it's bad,' said her mum quietly, sitting on the edge of the bed. 'I'm trying to sort it out, okay?'

We have to find out how to make him happy. We have to solve the mystery of how to keep him happy. We have to make everything perfect. When everything is perfect, he's happy.

'We have to leave,' Pip whispered. She wouldn't normally say something like that only her hand was aching and the aching made her feel reckless. 'We could take his car when he's at the pub.'

Her mum winced at that, bit her bottom lip.

We'll have a dragon, Pip wanted to add.

Was that Little Fella she could hear moving in the wardrobe?

'Shhh,' said her mother, touching her cheek. Then she was sighing and standing up.

'One more day of school, Pippa. And tomorrow you're *going* to school,' she said, turning the light out and closing the door.

Pip took Little Fella from the wardrobe in his hoodie nest and prepared her feeding equipment.

Yes, he was definitely a boy dragon. She had no proof of it, she just believed it. That's what happened with dragons. You started to believe stuff. Before a dragon, life had drifted. Information had washed over her. Times tables and Captain Cook, chewing gum advertisements and terrorism, all sorts of people blowing each other up, fidget spinners and fast cars, clean breath, Lego for girls and Lego for boys. Television and the chatter of the radio and Matt scrolling with his angry finger down the phone. With a dragon, she believed.

I will save you.

I will help you.

I will fix your wings.

I was chosen.

Chosen. It was such a huge word and she almost felt foolish thinking it. Maybe some other girl could have been sitting there at the creek, at dusk, and that other girl would have found him and saved him just as well. 'Chosen' was a weighty word.

She'd never in her whole life felt the weight of that word.

It made her feel like there were one hundred

Christmas mornings thrumming through her veins, excited and impatient.

She mushed arrowroot in the dark; he was hungry. He slurped and guzzled against the eye-dropper. He seemed bigger in the dark. She tentatively put her hand out and stroked his back. Those papery tufts felt rubbery now. He rattled beneath her fingers, writhed in a contented away.

'It'll be all right, Little Fella,' she whispered because she wasn't silly for thinking it. Because she believed it.

That first day in class, when Mika arrived and thrilled everyone with his solo travel escapades, he chose Pip. He could have become friends with any of the other boys. Those boys were there for the picking. There was Mason, Zane, Alex, Simon, Luke, Harry, Jack (times two), Hunter, Angus, Johnathan, Israel and Archie. And that was just her class. He talked to them of course and kicked the ball with them and argued with Hunter who everyone argued with, straightaway, and Angus, Alex and Simon gathered around him at recess when he extracted a mysterious battered magazine from his green backpack, the words 'The Unexplained' emblazoned on the front cover.

Maybe he noticed she wasn't really listening to the train story. That she was thinking of something else. Maybe he could see that, as he told the part about the dehydration. That she was staring out the window at the dead white grass. Maybe he saw her turn away when he showed the boys the article on werewolves. That she was a girl with things on her mind who needed a friend.

She had friends. That's what she thought, with annoyance, when he followed her home from school through the park. He was ten metres behind, head down, trudging in the heat with his backpack weighing him down. She had Emily, the funnier of the two twins, who made her laugh. She had Audrey, who sometimes invited her over to jump on her trampoline. She had Taliah, who commanded a large group of girls that sometimes Pip sat at the edge of. There were others too. Lots of other *sometimes* friends. She fitted in anywhere on the edges. She could blend. She was the blurred girl at the sides of photos, shapeshifting. Except with Laura Denning. She could *never* shapeshift with Laura.

Pip knew he was going to try to be her friend. He was going to try to fit in with her. She had a sense for such things. You had to wait for the right time and say the right thing. You had to get ready to disappear if it didn't work out. She could sense him waiting for the right time.

She had a flat tyre and she was glad for it. She was walking slowly, pushing her bike, because she didn't want to go home. Her mother would be thinking about what she'd make Matt for dinner and worrying that she had to make it right. If she didn't make it right Matt wouldn't talk to them. He'd go and turn his huge television up loud and pretend they didn't exist. He'd already done it twice since he'd moved in and Pip knew her mother never wanted it to happen again.

'You got a flat,' he said behind her.

'Uh huh,' she said.

'I can fix it,' he said, running to catch up. 'We need a bucket of water. Have you got one? I have a bike repair kit. You take the tube out and run it through the water looking for air bubbles.'

'I know how to fix a flat tyre.'

'Just saying,' he said. 'You got a bucket at home?'

He pulled the backpack around and rummaged. There seemed to be a lot of stuff in that bag. Finally, he retrieved the bike repair kit, a tiny plastic sleeve containing adhesives. He was beside her now.

'Why do you have that if you don't have a bike?'

'I had a bike,' he said. 'It was red with a thin white stripe. It belonged to this guy called Malcolm, then it was mine.'

'Okay,' she said slowly.

'But I had to leave it behind when I got put on the train in the middle of the night.'

In the park that first day, with some kind of sleight of hand, she ended up holding the tyre repair kit as he pushed her bike. No one had ever pushed her bike for her. She felt empty-handed, with the yellow grass crackling beneath her feet and the sun burning her cheeks.

'I think I can push my own bike,' she said.

'Mum had to run away. Like proper. But just for a while.'

'Run away? Why?'

'Our house was on Russell Street,' he said, ignoring that. 'Oxley. A really big backyard and in the big floods – you would have seen them on the telly – the water came right into the backyard. I had a trampoline. Well, it wasn't my trampoline, it belonged to my mum's friend Sharon's kids, we were looking after it. And the trampoline floated away.'

He laughed a little.

'I think it floated all the way out to sea.'

She didn't think that was possible but she didn't know him yet and she didn't want to argue with people she didn't know.

'It might even be as far as Sri Lanka.'

He didn't say anything for a while, letting her digest that image; a trampoline floating out over the ocean. Then, suddenly: 'My mother's car is a white Holden Commodore, registration number 966MOP. We used to laugh about that all the time. If you turn the first nine around you've got the devil's number.

It's pretty distinctive, right? Just in case you ever see it, you have to tell me straightaway. She's probably in Western Australia by now though. That's where she was heading and when it's safe, she will come and get me. Across the Nullarbor Plain. Have you ever been there?'

He dropped her bike suddenly, was unzipping his backpack again. He unfolded a crumpled piece of paper. It was a map of Australia, torn from somewhere, a dotted line drawn from Brisbane down through South Australia directly to the words: Nullarbor Plain.

'I've heard of it,' said Pip.

'I haven't been there yet but I reckon I'll go one day.'

That's what happened with Mika's stories. They started out one place and then expanded rapidly like the big bang and took you somewhere else altogether.

IT WAS A LONG NIGHT WITH LITTLE FELLA.
He woke every hour, rattled against her like a dry seed pod, and made a new noise, a low kind of mewling. To quiet him, she hurriedly mashed arrowroot into a gruel and fed him, sleeping when he slept, waking when he shifted against her. His little belly was plump. The tangle of broken wings sat upright on his back now, a mess filled with new life. They rustled and shivered. She thought his eyes might be opening a tiny slit.

Her palm ached. It was a deep ache. It throbbed, *lub, dub, lub, dub*, a heartbeat in her hand. It throbbed deep, then deeper, then deepest, as though that throb was a hole and she would fall into it and never climb out.

Then it eased, just as slowly, and sweat broke out on her forehead with relief. She heard Matt arrive home, tensed with the syringe in her hand, relaxed when she heard the television turn on.

In the morning, he was still asleep on the sofa, with the television on breakfast news, several beer bottles beside him. Her mum was in the kitchen scrolling.

Top fifty beef recipes simple tips to attain casual chic dinner recipes to keep your man happy how to get perfect skin luscious lips tips from the professionals perfect waves with the new pro-wave 300 five signs of emotional abuse take this quiz perfect body wash perfectly smooth skin six home remedies for bad breath secrets for perfect morning hair.

Pip tiptoed for her lunch box.

'Should I change the dressing?' whispered her mum, looking up.

'No, it's fine,' lied Pip. Her hand ached, slowly, methodically, never-endingly.

'Promise me,' said Mum.

'Of course, I'm going to school,' Pip whispered back.

She had her backpack on, a baby dragon sleeping inside it. Matt snored abruptly on the couch, a wild bear snore. He was going to wake up badly, Pip just knew it.

'I've got enough problems without having to worry about whether or not my daughter goes to school,' whispered her mother.

'I'm going to school,' said Pip.

She would keep her promise. She didn't know how but she would. She rode quickly down the street hoping she wouldn't meet anyone.

Archie was there at the crossing intersection, waiting.

'Did you get in trouble?' he asked, pedalling quick to catch up with her when she didn't stop.

'Yes,' she said.

'How much?'

'Heaps,' she said.

'My mum would lose it if I did that.'

Pip couldn't imagine Mrs Morgan losing it. Archie's mum was big but her smile was even more enormous. She worked at the tuckshop and she cracked jokes with the kids. She had a laugh that shook the tuckshop walls and sometimes they could hear it all the way from their classroom. Her laugh made them laugh, and when she laughed like that, Archie, who was theatrical, banged his head down onto his desk, which made the whole class laugh even more.

'Why'd you wag? Full truth,' he said. Archie could be intense. He cross-examined people like a lawyer.

'Stop being a busybody,' said Pip and straightaway that sounded uncool. 'I just didn't want to go. Seriously, it's one day to holidays, why do we even have to go to school?'

'Good point,' he said though he wasn't easily diverted. 'Then tell me what you did all day?'

'I did nothing.'

'Mum said you're probably still sad about Mika,' said Archie. 'Everyone is. You still got to go to school, Pip.'

Pip wasn't expecting that. Her cheeks prickled all over.

'Shut up,' was all she could say as she took off, standing up to pedal fast to get away from him.

'Pip,' he called after her as she rode as fast as she could.

When she looked back though, he wasn't even trying to catch her.

*S*HE HADN'T MISSED ANYTHING AT SCHOOL.
Same boys kicking balls on the oval. Same flies
hanging around their lunch boxes. The same heat,
shimmering on the parade ground. Christmas card
making was still waiting for her. The stack of Christmas
card photocopies were there on Mr T's desk. There
were some sad, half-dry glitter pens in a margarine
container and some mangy glue sticks.

There was Mika's desk and chair, still empty in the
corner like he might come back.

'Miss Pippa,' said Mr T. 'Welcome back.'

She'd left her backpack in the port rack, a dragon
inside it. She'd brought that dragon back from the brink

of death. She'd been awake nearly all night because it wouldn't stop eating. Her palm was throbbing violently. She didn't have time for Mr T.

'Hi,' said Pip, dragging out her chair. Mr T flinched at the scraping noise it made.

'Sorry.'

Laura Denning turned to stare at her, twirling her long blonde ponytail.

'What happened to your hand?' she demanded. That's what Laura Denning did. Demanded to know what was going on. Demanded people pay attention to her. Demanded people know she had the best lunch box in school. Demanded they play the games she wanted to play.

'None of your business,' said Pip.

'What have you done to your hand?' asked Mr T, two seconds later.

'Fell on some rocks.'

Her hand was burning, a camp fire right there in her palm. The burning started low like embers and grew until she was holding the sun in her hand. When it died down, she could think again. Mr T's voice faded away each time the burning resumed. Each time she held the sun in her hand the rest of her grew cold. She was nothing but a shivery inconsequential ghost attached to that hand.

It had only been a day and a half since she found the dragon, yet they felt like the longest days of her life. She had to peer way into the past to see the moment she found Little Fella in the creek. Even sitting in the cave seemed in the distant past, like she was viewing it all through a telescope. They had been like the days in a legend.

Everything seemed small. The world had shrunk. Or at least the world she knew. She figured it was because the part she didn't know had grown even vaster. Behind the red hills, a dragon had flown and it had lost its baby and she knew she'd have to return it.

At recess, after Mr T blew the whistle to announce the beginning of playtime, she grabbed her backpack and headed to the oval to sit under a tree. She tried not to seem suspicious, moving away from people. She tried to act natural, like she just wanted to sit under one of the weeping silvery eucalypts and have some downtime. Sitting alone always caused trouble at school though. People always needed reasons for such behaviour. Girls like Laura Denning or the Cartwright twins were the sitting alone police. *Are you being bullied? Are you feeling sad? Is it about Mika?*

She glanced around her, as casually as possible: no Laura, no Cartwright twins, the boys on the far side of the oval kicking the football. The schoolyard sounds faded. She opened the zipper a fraction and heard Little Fella rattle.

'I'm sorry about this Little Fella,' she said, hurriedly mushing arrowroot with water. She checked again that no one was watching, and then placed the syringe down into the backpack to feed him.

He slurped loudly. Made the surprising mewling sound.

'Shhhh, Little Fella,' she said.

Another syringe-full, as quickly as she could so he would quiet down. He slurped even louder. Syringe after syringe. She peered into the dark interior of the bag to see if his eyes were open but they were closed. She knew they'd open soon. Knew it in her heart, in her guts. Catching a glimpse of his dark scales, the terrible rushing heart inflation started up, and tears flooded her eyes. The palm of her left hand exploded into a deep ache that took minutes to subside.

'Ouch!' She glanced away quickly. 'Geez, Little Fella, why are you so hungry?'

Gradually he grew tired. He rattled in a softer, sleepier way. The bell rang for the end of recess.

'What you got in there?' asked Archie quietly on the way back to class.

His brown arms were sweaty and he was breathless. He'd been playing footy.

'Pardon?' said Pip.

'What's in your backpack?' He was smiling his big Archie smile but, thankfully, talking quietly. 'Is it the *something* you were taking *somewhere*?'

'There's nothing in my backpack,' she replied and kept walking.

'You're so sprung, Pip,' he said. 'I saw it. Don't deny it.'

He was louder now and there were other kids around them, moving past them towards the covered verandah.

'What did you see?' she hissed.

'I saw you feeding something.'

'I wasn't feeding anything.'

'Baby joey?' he asked. It wasn't unheard of. The twins brought one to school once in a calico sack for show and tell.

'Nope,' she said.

'Baby possum?'

'Nope. Nothing in my backpack.'

'You're so gammin, Pip,' he said.

A FEW MORE HOURS. THAT'S ALL SHE HAD to get through. *You can do this,* she told herself, silently, trying to hear above the pain in her left palm that was pounding, like waves, pummelling a shore. They had to make Christmas cards. *Yay,* she said to herself, deadpan.

A few more hours and school would be done. Little Fella was asleep in the backpack on the hot port rack. Surely, he would sleep until next break.

Just a few more hours.

Just a few more hours.

Just a few more hours.

Her palm burned bright and then dimmed. Bright, dim. Bright, dim. Lighthouse Pip. Maybe she was sending a message to the mother dragon with her ache. Maybe she was turning into a beacon. She shivered as she sat back in her classroom chair. But the shiver was far, far away, as though it was happening to a memory of herself.

Archie caught her gaze from three desks down.

'What is it?' he mouthed.

She ignored him.

Laura Denning turned back to stare at her again.

'What did he say?' she demanded.

'I don't know, ask him,' said Pip.

Laura Denning rolled her eyes.

What if the dragon scratch changed me? It was a thought that was suddenly on repeat in her head. She tried to shake it loose, but the thought went around and around like a Ferris wheel, and with each turn her stomach lurched.

'Okay, now for the fun part of the day. We're going to make some cards,' said Mr T and everyone cheered half-heartedly. 'Come on, guys!'

There were two templates to choose from. A simple 'HO HO HO' or a reindeer with a red nose.

Seriously, said Mika in her head. *What kind of choice is that?*

I know.

Pip looked at his empty desk and chair.

'What did you say?' demanded Laura Denning.

'I didn't say anything, did I?' said Pip.

'You said "I know".'

'Oh.'

The Ferris wheel went around fast, a full spin.

'You okay, Pippa?' asked Mr T.

Her vision was blurred but there he was in the distance, far away, at the front of the class, handing out glitter pens. Her hand burned bright, dimmed.

'Yes, I'm good,' she whispered.

Archie caught her eye again.

'What was it?' he mouthed.

She looked away.

Laura Denning was unhappy with her glitter pen colour. 'Ho Ho Ho or a reindeer?' asked Mr T. Someone shut their tidy tray loudly, *bang*, like a clap of thunder in her brain. Archie raised his eyebrows. Far away at the tuckshop his mother laughed. The sun shoved its face right up to the louvres and baked them.

'There's only one HO HO HO left!'

What if the scratch changed me?

The Ferris wheel jolted; her stomach flipped. Now that thought just sat there and expanded. It was stuck in her head like a coin in a slot.

She felt changed.

Altered.

Her cheeks were hot and her blood felt different.

What if there was magic in that scratch? Not Disney magic. Not stars and talking birds. What if it was something terrible and dark? What if she grew wings? What if they started pushing out of her skin, like black knitting needles? She imagined the pain and then realised that she actually had pain in her back. Bad pain, right beneath her shoulder blades.

Mr T handed her the last HO HO HO card.

'Are you sure you're okay, Pip?'

'Yes,' she said, then she stood up in the middle of the class and vomited.

IT WAS A GOOD THING, THAT VOMIT. SHE TOLD herself that. Although the twenty-three shocked faces were not. She had vomited all over her desk and her ruler and erasers and then all over the floor. Another wave came soon after and splashed Laura Denning right on her light-up sneakers.

It was a good thing.

She would get to go home.

She was led from the classroom out into the fresh air and to her backpack that contained a dragon and all the way to the sick bay at D verandah with Mrs Green. Laura Denning had to be escorted there too because she was so shocked to have spew all over her light-up sneakers.

Pip wanted to say, *I'm sorry Laura*, but she had no words, she could only shiver. She sat on her sick bay bed with her backpack beside her while Mrs Green removed Laura's sneakers and assisted her to lie down.

'You need to calm down,' Mrs Green said sternly, because Laura was sobbing and hiccupping and she'd gone blotchy all over her face.

Who even wears light-up sneakers when they're ten? Pip wanted to ask, but she couldn't. She shivered instead, a giant shiver, that rattled the rickety old sick bay bed. Mrs Green would be cranky at her if she said something like that.

Anyway, she'd never see Mrs Green again.

She'd never see Grade Five or Mr T again. Pip knew it suddenly, right then.

That made her head swim. She let out a small gasp.

'Are you going to be sick again? You've gone very pale,' said Mrs Green.

'I . . .' said Pip. It was all she could manage before she shuddered again.

'That's impressive,' Mrs Green said when the thermometer beeped. 'I'm going to ring your mother straightaway.'

She was almost through the door when she stopped. 'What was that sound?'

Pip wanted to say, *I don't know*, but shivered violently instead. Of course, she knew. It was the sound of a baby dragon that needed feeding.

It was the rattling sound.

The maraca sound.

The mewling sound.

All three listened into the quiet. Little Fella was quiet in return, listening to them.

Please, please, please, please, please, Pip wished for him to stay quiet.

Mrs Green frowned and left the room.

When she was gone, Pip watched Laura Denning who was staring at the ceiling, very pale, trying to stop crying. Pip dragged her backpack towards her and opened the zipper a fraction. Little Fella was peering up at her, his eyes open for the very first time. They were black, not at all what she'd expected, and she stifled another small gasp. Little Fella hissed and rattled, though not in a bad way. It was a very friendly hiss and rattle. An I'd-like-some-arrowroot-biscuit-mush rattle.

Pip quickly closed the zip as Mrs Green appeared at the door again.

'Your mum is coming in a minute,' said Mrs Green, handing her an ice-cream bucket. 'In case you feel like you're going to vomit again.'

'Can I wait out front for her?' Finally some words. Pip was surprised to hear her voice. *It's me*, she thought. *I'm still me. I'm not changed yet.*

'No, your mum can come up to fetch you.'

'I think I need fresh air,' shuddered Pip, 'or I'm going to spew.'

'Okay, but sit on the top step until you see her pull up,' said Mrs Green. 'And I want to talk to her.'

'Goodbye Laura,' said Pip. 'I'm really sorry.'

Laura didn't reply. She began crying dramatically again.

It wasn't that much spew on your sneakers, Pip wanted to say.

*S*HE REALLY HAD EXPECTED TOXIC GREEN eyes. Or cool blue like the iceblocks they sold at the tuckshop. Not dark and filmy. Little Fella's eyes were the colour of a kitten's eyes when they first opened. Blank. When he'd lifted his snout in that backpack, she knew he couldn't see her properly yet. He was very young.

She thought about these things until the taxi pulled up, her mum in the passenger seat. The inside of the taxi smelled of heated up vinyl and the taxidriver looked suspiciously at Pip and her ice-cream bucket.

'Goodbye Mrs Green,' said Pip after Mrs Green had told her mum about the temperature.

'Goodbye darling. See you in the new year,' said Mrs Green.

But Pip knew she wouldn't.

Pip talked loudly the whole way home in case Little Fella rattled or mewled again. She talked about the spew and Laura's reaction and Laura's light-up sneakers until her mum, embarrassed, said, 'Pip, why are you talking so loud?'

'I don't know,' said Pip.

'It must be the fever.'

In her bedroom she breathed a sigh of relief and mushed biscuits quickly while her mother made a doctor's appointment. There were only three biscuits left and that worried her. The dragon sniffed the air and mewled.

'Hush, Little Fella,' Pip said. 'Quickly.'

Even though she was aching and burning she felt a surge of love as he lifted his snout to suck at the syringe. It was seismic, that billowing swell in her heart – the force of it could catapult her into outer space.

Faraway, she heard her mother say, 'She has some kind of infection in her hand, I think. She got a scratch.'

Pip pulled the blanket over Little Fella, brazenly, when her mother came in. She lifted her knees. He'd had six full syringes, so he was quieter, but she knew it was dangerous. One rattle, one hiss, and he'd be discovered.

'We can't get in until four,' said her mum.

'It's okay. I don't think I really need to go; I feel much better.'

'You don't look right, Pippa. You're a funny colour.'

That made Pip freeze.

'What colour am I?'

She imagined her skin turning dark like a bruised banana, a stain of darkness spreading over her, scales too.

'Pale. Really pale.'

'I'll have a little sleep,' said Pip.

Her mother was leaning over now to touch her head. Pip hoped Little Fella didn't move or make a noise. Her heart galloped.

'You're not as hot,' said her mum. 'That's good. Yes, have a sleep, Little Swan, you've got hours and hours.'

Little Swan. Her mother hadn't called her that in years.

Little Swan was a name from before Matt, when it

was just the two of them. When her mum was allowed to eat sushi and save spiders not squish them and sing songs from the nineties. When she dreamed of studying marine biology.

Little Swan. Pip wanted to say the words.

But her mum looked sad for saying them; she was turning already, swallowing them down, and heading towards the bedroom door.

Pip uncovered Little Fella. He rattled and lifted his snout. She fed him the last of the mushed biscuits and then rummaged at the bottom of the bag, taking out a tin of spaghetti. She opened the ring pull and placed a strand of spaghetti near the corner of Little Fella's mouth.

It was a messy affair.

'Suck,' she whispered. 'Suck, Little Fella.'

He opened his mouth, waiting for the syringe.

'You've got to slurp it in,' she whispered. His black eyes turned towards her voice.

She placed the strand into his mouth and this time the spaghetti disappeared and the force of it almost pulled her finger in as well.

Schlupp.

In slid another strand.

She tried again. He was waiting this time. *Schlupp.* Another and then another. She giggled and Little Fella lifted his snout wanting more.

Schlupp.

Schlupp.

Schlupp.

She laughed out loud and then shushed herself, in case her mother heard. She listened for Mika. It would have cracked him up, her hands covered in tomato sauce, a tiny dragon slurping spaghetti. He would have laughed his Mika laugh, with his eyes shut and one pale arm across his belly.

'Mika,' she whispered his name and it sounded different on her tongue.

Mick. Ahhh.

'How come you only show up sometimes?' she whispered.

No answer.

'Fine then,' she said.

Little Fella ate the third-last strand of spaghetti,

shivered and stretched. He ate the second-last strand and his eyelids grew heavy. And while he ate the very last piece, his eyes closed. He slurped one last time, made a small sighing noise, rattled, curled himself tight into a ball.

Pip sighed too. She shivered and scooped him up and carried him to the wardrobe.

WHEN MIKA CAME TO SCHOOL IN THE LAST
days of Grade Three, he upset the natural order
of things. An extra desk had to be found for him and
squished in beside Laura Denning and she didn't like that.
She slid her Hello Kitty pencil case away from his side
and seemed annoyed. At recess Laura told him she didn't
think the story of his train trip was true. 'Who even goes
on trains these days anyway?' she said, looking around
her for support. The covered eating area was strangely
quiet. She asked him where he *really* came from.

Mika smiled at her.

'Do you really want to know?' he asked. 'Do you
really, really, really want to know?'

She scowled at him. She was all pink ribbons and pouty strawberry-scented lip gloss.

He was all shaggy white-blonde hair and boniness.

He leaned in close and whispered.

'I come from beyond the black hole of Sagittarius A.'

That made all the boys laugh out loud. And Laura even angrier.

'You're full of it up to here,' she pointed to her neck.

Pip, sitting on the edges, looked at the concrete and tried not to smile.

Friends moved away from friends to be near him. Various boys tried to claim him straightaway and so did many of the girls. Usually new kids were quiet and unsure; they needed to be buddied up with someone chosen by the teacher. Not Mika. He behaved like he'd done this before.

He had. He'd been to seven schools. He said *SEVEN* like it was a magical number. This was his *SEVENTH* school. He was new and exciting and he talked a lot. He had more stories, better stories than the train story. Science fiction stories. Supernatural stories. Black hole stories. Man-eating plant stories.

Stories about spontaneous human combustion. A story about a man he knew who once saw a ghost in a house in Taringa.

So, when he was sitting on her front steps with her at the end of that first day, one patch missing from his tyre-fixing pack, Pip felt even stranger than those stories.

Pip.

Edge-sitter.

Shapeshifter.

Sometimes friend-haver.

Why was he with her? That was definitely a crumbling of the natural order of things.

On her front steps he told her his old house had a secret passage.

'What for?' she said. Trying to not sound too excited.

'For getaways,' Mika said.

This passage ran between the bathroom and the laundry. He could crawl through a door beneath the bathroom sink and the passage twisted and turned twice and then came out in the laundry beneath the sink there.

'It was the best place in the world and whenever I remembered it, when I was in a pinch, I was like, *yes*, we have a secret passage. Like you know when you wake up from a bad dream and realise it was only a dream? Pip, that's what it was like remembering that secret passage.'

She liked the way he said her name.

Like he'd always known her.

She wanted to know what he was getting away from in those secret passages but she didn't like to ask. To be honest, in the park she hadn't wanted him to catch up or to try to fit in with her yet now she didn't want to say anything that might make him not like her. She didn't want to seem too excited or not excited enough.

Her mother came to the front patio when she heard their voices.

'Hello,' she said to Mika. 'Haven't seen you before.'

'I'm brand spanking new,' said Mika, which made her laugh.

'Do you two want some bickies?' she asked.

There was still lots of Pip's old mum showing then, apart from the worrying about getting dinner wrong.

She was jumpy though nowhere near as jumpy as she'd become. She was still allowed to go to her art classes and look at holiday package deals and speak to most people. She seemed happy that Pip had a friend on her front steps.

Mika munched his way through three biscuits but the getaway question was still inside Pip's mouth as she chewed.

'What did you have to get away from?' she asked at last, when he was about to leave. One foot in her yard, the other out. She didn't want him to go. Matt would be home soon and she'd have to disappear to her bedroom. She'd have to return to pretending she didn't exist.

'Get away?' he asked.

'In the secret passage?'

'Oh,' he sighed. 'Tell you tomorrow, Pip, when we walk to school.'

She stood at her front gate as the natural order of things completely disintegrated, and smiled.

'I can show you a waterhole I know,' she said. 'After school. If you like.'

'**A**LL RIGHTY THEN, WHAT'S UNDERNEATH this bandage?' asked the doctor.

'I scratched myself on spinifex.'

'Have you looked at it today?' he asked, un-bandaging it.

'Last night,' said Mum.

'All righty then, we could have an infection here. She's certainly got a temperature.'

Pip watched the doctor examining her hand. *All righty then. Awl. Rye. Tee. Thin.* Everyone's voices were weird. They kept breaking up in her head, like a radio with static. She hoped Little Fella was okay. He hadn't woken again after the tinned spaghetti.

She hoped tinned spaghetti wasn't toxic to small dragons.

The doctor prescribed her antibiotics. He whispered to her mother while Pip sat on the leather examination table. She tried to catch what the doctor was saying but his voice was unexpectedly soft, like a snake slipping through grass.

Single words snapped into pieces.

Ye. sssss. Nor. mal. Tra. Ged. eeeee.

'What did he whisper to you?' she asked her mother when they were outside.

'He just told me to keep a good eye on you. What do you feel like for dinner?'

'Arrowroot biscuits?' she said, no hesitation. 'Packets and packets and packets.'

It made her mum laugh, her old laugh, and despite her aching hand, it made Pip feel happy.

'Arrowroot biscuits it is then. Do you want to sit on the bench?

'No, I feel fine,' said Pip.

Fine, she said to herself in the grocery shop. But she wasn't. For a start, 'fine' sounded strange in her head too, the 'f' of 'fine' as abrasive as a scourer. It made her shudder. The shop seemed different and her hand ached in response. She could see the reflection of the ceiling in the polished tile floor. She'd never noticed that before. She was suddenly wary of the shadows beneath the shelves. She could hear the fluoro lights humming. The fridges too, talking and rumbling amongst themselves.

The checkout beeps rang out loud as bells.

'You grab the arrowroots,' her mum said. 'I'll get a few things.'

In the biscuit aisle Pip searched for the arrowroots. She picked up three packets and hoped her mother still thought it was funny.

She didn't. She shook her head.

'It's a simple food,' said Pip. 'I only feel like simple foods.'

Simple. Pimple. Dimple.

Sim-pull. Pim-pull. Dim-pull.

At the counter, Pip watched the cashier's skin. It was a strange colour, human skin. There was a pulse in the cashier's throat and if she listened close enough, she could almost hear it. Something was happening to Pip and she wasn't sure what. She really hoped the antibiotics changed her back to who she had been.

She waited at the end of the checkout while her mother packed the groceries in her bag. Soon they'd be out of that place, which seemed suddenly way too loud. The checkout bells and footsteps and fridges talking and people's voices rumbling, rumbling, rumbling. And in amongst it all someone was saying her name.

Pip. Pip. Pip.

A tiny sound, like pebbles hitting a metal can.

That name didn't even mean anything. Not really. She knew that, right there in that cool shady grocery store where everything hummed and sighed and the pulse ticked in the checkout lady's throat. Her name was just a tiny bandaid over the vastness of her.

It was Laura Denning standing near the trolleys and the gumball machine. She was with her mother who had her back turned, a baby on her hip, talking to two other women with babies on their hips.

'I've been saying your name for ages,' said Laura.

'I didn't hear you, that's all,' said Pip. 'I was . . .'

'Deep in thought,' said Laura.

She wasn't wearing her light-up sneakers, Pip noticed. Laura noticed her noticing.

'In the bin,' she explained.

'Sorry,' said Pip. 'I was at the doctor's. I have an infection in my hand.'

She held up the new white bandage and Laura momentarily seemed impressed.

She'd like to really impress Laura. She'd like to say, *Laura Denning, you don't know the half of it.*

Laura wasn't her friend. They were as different as two people could possibly get. Laura would never dig in the creek with a stick. Pip would never wear light-up sneakers. Laura Denning would have a Barbie townhouse in her bedroom. Pip would stake her whole life on that prediction. Girls like Laura had Barbie townhouses and Barbie campervans even when they were in Grade Five. She'd have a palace pet collection and somewhere in her wardrobe there'd be an old Elsa costume.

They stared at each other, thinking these things. Though Pip couldn't be sure, really, of what Laura was thinking. She was probably feeling repulsed by Pip, remembering the vomit or something. She looked uneasy. Why did she even call Pip over? Now it was just a mess and she'd have to extricate herself from it.

Laura Denning leaned in really quickly and whispered in Pip's ear.

'What was in your bag?'

'What?' said Pip, as though she didn't hear.

'You had something in your bag, making a noise. And it stunk. Some kind of creature.'

She said that all so quickly into her ear that it made Pip feel dizzy.

'No, I didn't,' Pip said.

'I saw,' said Laura.

'I SAW.' EYE SAW. EYE SORE. ALL THE WAY HOME in the taxi Laura's words were stuck in Pip's ear. Her mum had the taxidriver take them through the drive-through at the bottle shop and bought herself some wine. *Saw I. Saw Eye. Sore Eye.* Her palm sent out flashlight beams of pain into the universe. The man at the bottle shop knew her mother.

'What happened to your little Corolla?' he asked.

'We're trying to save for a house,' her mum lied, 'so you know, it's the whole one car thing at the moment. And he's at work.'

'For sure,' said the man, nodding like he understood.

Then, laughing, 'Big cricket weekend coming up. Matt will be on the beers.'

Like drinking lots of beers was absolutely hilarious.

Pip's mum laughed too, as though it was the funniest thing she'd heard.

She said, 'I probably won't see him until Sunday afternoon, will I?'

That wasn't true. *If only*, thought Pip.

'You okay?' her mum asked as they got back on the highway. She touched Pip's forehead. 'You're burning up again.'

'I really want to sleep.'

At home, her mother gave her two of the new pink pills and some Panadol. She asked how many biscuits Pip wanted.

'A whole packet.'

'Don't be silly, Pippa.'

She was given a plate containing eight thickly buttered arrowroots. She didn't know if butter was okay for Little Fella. Maybe dragons were lactose-intolerant. And she hoped he wouldn't smell them all the way from the bedroom. She hadn't heard anything since they arrived home but maybe the arrowroots would make him start up his mewling.

'Can I eat them in bed?'

'Of course,' said her mother. Her face was kind yet impatient. Scared yet resigned. Happy yet sad. It was Friday night, after all. Anything could happen on a Friday night. Matt and the pub. Her mother and wine. A dragon in her wardrobe.

Pip started singing as soon as she shut her bedroom door. She hadn't known that song was even there. She tried to not think about it this time. It just was. She was definitely changing and there was nothing she could do about it. And maybe it wouldn't be something bad, anyway.

It felt inevitable. Like the sun going down.

There were the tears as well; they were already on her cheeks as she walked towards the wardrobe, like in the cave yesterday, dripping steadily. He was waiting. Dark, blind eyes, searching for her song.

She took him in her arms, wrapped in his hoodie nest, and sat on the bed. She sang to Little Fella in the late afternoon light, feeding him mushed-up biscuit.

It was a strange humming song, made up of parts of words.

Little Fella wasn't dried out like a toad skin anymore. He was plump with a little belly. His head had filled out too, his black scales smooth. She ran her fingers over his belly, and he twitched. She touched each and every claw as though she were remembering them. The little rubbery nubs on his nose were firm and the tufts of papery stuff stood upright. She touched the rumpled mess that were his wings.

She was changing so he could change. She knew that much.

He couldn't stand yet, although he was doing something with his back legs like he might be going to try. He was wriggling them, shifting them, trying to move towards her, bumping his head against the back of her palm.

I saw.

'It's okay, it's okay,' Pip sang in that other language, although she knew that's what the song said. 'We'll never see Laura Denning again.'

Outside her window, the sun was slipping and the galahs were flooding across the sky towards the creek and the tears dried on her cheeks. She left him there on her bed, sleeping.

She found her mother sitting on the back steps, staring at her withered roses. Pip's rosebush was called Double Delight and her mum's was called Piccadilly. She'd planted them years before and Pip could remember when she was small, those roses filling vases and teacups. Now the bushes were brown, skeletal, only the tiniest hint of green in the petals. Clinging to life.

'Let me feel your head again,' her mother said.

Pip sat down beside her.

'Still hot,' said her mum. 'Have you been crying?'

'A bit,' said Pip. 'Not much.'

Her eyes must have been puffy.

'Sorry,' said her mum. She put her arm around Pip.

'You don't have to be sorry,' said Pip. 'What are you sorry for?'

'Stuff,' said her mum.

Pip shook her head. She really wanted to tell her mother. She really wanted to say, *Look, I have a dragon in my wardrobe. I'm saving it. It scratched me and I think it's changing me. I don't know how but not in a bad way, so I don't want you to worry.*

'I'm ringing Mum in a minute,' said her mother. 'See if we can maybe go there.'

'For the holidays?'

'Yes . . . maybe for longer,' said her mum. She whispered the last part. As though just saying it, he'd hear her. Even though he was ages away, down a hole, underground.

They weren't allowed to ring Pip's grandmother if Matt was there. He said she was a 'crazy' woman. A menace. A meddler. Really, she wasn't. Pip knew it and she knew her mum knew it.

Pip stared at the sky and thought of the dragon who'd lost her baby.

'What do you think?' said her mum.

Once they'd been planning a holiday to her grandmother's house, but Matt had talked Pip's mum out of it. He'd said she mustn't care that much about him if she'd just up and leave for a holiday like that. If she looked at snorkelling holidays at the Great Barrier

Reef, he'd say they'd go one day except they had other more important things to pay off first. Like his four-wheel drive.

And the time they *had* gone, when her mum said she was leaving Matt, he'd come and got them back. He'd driven all night through the desert and across the Great Dividing Range and parked outside Pip's grandmother's house in Townsville and begged her mum to come back. And everything that had been good had been undone in a matter of minutes.

'I think you should ring her,' said Pip.

Pip's grandmother kept joeys in pillowcases and possums in boxes. Pip felt a rush of excitement, imagining what her grandmother would think of Little Fella.

She checked herself just as quickly. It was better not to get too excited. They'd been going before then never gone.

'Okay,' said her mum. 'I'll come check on you later.'

'You don't need to,' said Pip. 'The pills are working, I think. Will you really ring?'

'Yes,' whispered her mum. 'Soon.'

Inside, the pantry door was open. The arrowroots sitting right there. She took a packet. In the junk drawer Pip found sticky tape, paddle-pop sticks, rubber bands. Her grandmother would have much better creature-saving medical supplies.

She closed her bedroom door and her hand throbbed, although her skin was cold. She took Little Fella from the wardrobe and pushed him a little way beneath the blanket then climbed in beside him, shivering.

'I'll fix your wings,' she promised. She knew she would. Like a tide. Like a river running. Like the moon rising. 'But first we need to sleep.'

She listened for Mika's voice in her head, her eyes closed. There was only silence.

Please don't go yet, she said to him.

'I**T'S AN OASIS,' MIKA SAID WHEN HE FIRST**
saw the waterhole, which made Pip laugh because
it wasn't. It was just a small pond filled with dark water
that always remained after the river ran. It never dried
up. It was only a couple of metres wide, surrounded by
grass that had more colour than any of the other grasses
in the area, and that was it.

It wasn't an oasis. It wasn't shady. The sun could
burn the hair right off your head if you sat there in
the middle of the day. One side of the waterhole
was raised into a small hillock and there was a fallen
silvery log, washed smooth by countless seasons of
the rivers running, that served as a seat. The top

of the water was hot to touch, cool beneath. It was *her* place.

That first day at the waterhole Mika raised his hand and closed his eyes. It was the first time she'd seen him do that. He announced that he suspected a bunyip lived in its depths.

'What even is a bunyip?' she'd asked.

'A scary creature that lives in outback waterholes,' he replied.

She knew that. She wanted details. She took her school shoes off and slipped her feet through the top layer of hot water and into the cool. Her legs were sepia-coloured through the water. A brown hawk circled lazily, high above in the sky.

'Gee, I hope I don't get eaten,' she said and smiled at him.

He didn't take his shoes off but sat on the small bank beside her.

'They have very sharp teeth,' he said.

'It must like me, it's never bitten.'

'Have you ever swum in there? Can you touch the bottom?'

'Not game,' said Pip. She wasn't embarrassed to admit it. 'They reckon it has no bottom. My mum said that. Some waterholes are like that, especially if they never dry up.'

'I wonder if Gran knows about it,' he said, frowning. 'She grew up here.'

He took a yellow torch from his backpack and shone its weak light into the water.

'I think torches work better at night,' said Pip, wondering what else he had in that backpack.

'I know!' he cried and then, smiling again, he was up looking for something, rushing towards the opposite side of the river where the gums grew.

'What are you doing?' she called.

'We need a stick. A *really* long stick,' he called back.

She removed her feet from the water. He was going to need help. He was a city boy, after all. She walked across the dry riverbed, the silt scales cracking in a satisfying way beneath her bare feet.

The tree limb they found required two to carry it and they had to walk a way along the bulldust road that ran on the hill side of the river to find it. When the river had run the stick must have snapped from its mother tree and wedged there between two old silver gums. It was taller than both of them put together and they grunted under the weight of it and the grunting made them laugh so much they had to stop several times. By the time they had it back at the waterhole the sun was already starting its slide.

They positioned it so that they could slip it into the dark water but then Mika stopped. He was doubled over with the exertion.

'What if we annoy the bunyip?' he said.

'I didn't carry it all this way to not do it,' said Pip, panting.

They broke the surface of the water and plunged the tree limb down, down into the water. It didn't stop. Both of them held it and kept pushing and it kept going, the small dark pool swallowing that stick like it had no problems with that at all until all that they had left was their hands holding the tree limb near the surface and still they felt no resistance.

'Yeah, that's deep,' said Mika as they heaved it back out. The surface of the pool wobbled and then returned to reflecting the glowing afternoon sky. They leaned forwards and stared at themselves.

Mika drew a spiral in the water with his fingertip, sighed.

'Told you so,' said Pip.

SHE UNRAVELLED THE WINGS AND IN HER
dream it was easy. Her fingers were made for it.
She unfurled sections with nothing but the tips of her
fingers; she stretched them out and smoothed them,
barely touching. She sang to those wings, a wing-
mending song. She was so glad she remembered that
song.

It was her mum calling out that woke her. It was
dark.

'Don't,' she heard her say. 'Don't.'

'Do *not* call me that!' she heard her mother shout
quite clearly.

Then the heavy sound of Matt's feet.

Sitting bolt upright, Pip listened over the top of her heartbeat. She felt for Little Fella who slept on beside her.

Matt was talking, a low stream of words, a rumble of words, like stones. They were meant to hurt.

'Don't!' her mum cried. Pip flinched and the dragon raised his head in the dark.

A small thud followed by another, louder. Footsteps, the television going on. Loud television. The great roar of race cars exploded down the hallway.

Her door opened and in the dark, she heard her mother's breathing.

'Are you okay?' Pip whispered.

'Yes,' said her mother. 'Everything's okay. Are you okay?'

'I'm okay.'

But everything was *not* okay.

Lights had come on in the street and dogs were barking. The race car engines were screaming. Matt was made completely out of anger. He wore an armour of anger and he had anger blood and he had a heart that was solid anger. He couldn't be broken.

He was made of titanium. Even if he were smashed to pieces, he'd just be hard bits of metal. Everything was *not* okay.

She hoped it was over.

That he'd fall asleep on the sofa. That he'd fall asleep like an ogre in a fairytale.

That he'd never wake up. No one would ever come and kiss him. There was no potion that could bring him back. She hated that thought and that thought hated her and she couldn't stop her heart from jack-hammering in her chest.

They needed to go to Townsville to her grandmother and grandfather's house.

They had to.

She'd hope for it. Even though she'd given up hoping before, she'd start hoping again. She'd hope for it with all her might and, somehow, she'd make it happen like hoping was a magic spell.

She turned on her torch and shone it at Little Fella's wings. The little dragon opened his eyes in the dark, and Pip saw a tiny flash of amber inside them. A zing. A little lightning strike.

'Hey,' she whispered. 'I knew you wouldn't have black eyes.'

Her heart slowed gradually.

She had to be careful with the torch; too much movement and maybe Matt would see it flickering under her door. That would be the kind of thing that would make him go off. He'd grab that torch and snap it in two.

She touched Little Fella's wing gently to see how he would react. He watched her, another little amber zing in his eye. She knew it was the right time. He knew it was the right time. It was the only time.

Only, fixing those wings was nothing like in the dream. It was like unravelling contact paper. Just to make it even more difficult her hand ached and her skin burned and then grew cold. The heat flushed up from her hand, up her arm, into her chest, then receded, leaving her to quiver.

Each wave of heat and she wondered if she was glowing.

Pip, the beacon.

Pip, the lighthouse.

She set up her equipment. The paddle-pop sticks and sticky tape.

'You're being so good, Little Fella,' she whispered.

She didn't know how long it took her. At some point she was aware that the car race was over, the house in silence, then suddenly, the sound of Matt, bumping off the walls, down the hallway towards the bedroom. Pip froze but there was no more shouting.

Maybe hours passed. The sun was already starting to flush against her bedroom door by the time she was finished. Where there were breaks in the rubbery sinew of the wings, she attached the paddle-pop sticks, six in total. Little Fella lay there with those messed-up wings outstretched while she worked. He slept. He woke. She fed him arrowroot biscuit mush. He slept again.

She had to be sure that he could refold the wings with the paddle-pop sticks in place so she had to restart, several times. He let her fold and unfold, occasionally rattling in a disgruntled way. There were tiny tears everywhere in the wings themselves and she covered them over, top and bottom, with sticky tape, hoping they would mend. Sometimes, quite suddenly, she sang softly, and cried tears over him. They were quick songs, though, like little storms. When they'd passed, she felt better for it.

'There you go, Little Fella,' she said when she was done. She yawned, admiring her handiwork. He folded up his wings, paddle-pop sticks and all, curled himself tight. Pip curled around him, surrounded by a litter of paddle-pop and sticky tape snippings.

They'd escape. They'd make it to Townsville. Her mother, her, Little Fella.

'Everything will be okay,' she whispered.

When the morning came the house was quiet and in the quiet Little Fella's belly gurgled. Pip carried him quickly to the back door, opened it silently, raced down the steps and placed him in the rose garden.

'Wow,' she said, at the smell. 'That's bad, Little Fella.'

The next-door neighbour's dog growled on the chain.

She tiptoed into the kitchen in search of more dragon food. Couscous? Instant rice? She decided against those. Bananas, baked beans, tinned custard. Her hand lingered, the tin disappeared into her dressing gown pocket. The Weet-Bix box.

Turned out he was a little Weet-Bix-eating monster. She mushed up a second bowl in her bedroom and wondered what dragons ate in the wild. Not Weet-Bix and biscuits, that's for sure. She wondered if he would breathe fire. There hadn't been any hint of fire yet although that morning he was snuffling a lot and maybe that was what dragons did in preparation. If he started breathing fire that was probably going to be a problem.

He had managed to get his back legs to work. He was able to climb into a sitting position, his little snout nudging her Weet-Bix hand. There were more zings of copper and bronze and amber in his eyes this morning too. They flashed and faded and each time she couldn't help a little involuntary gasp.

He snuffled and rattled and hissed and mewled for more Weet-Bix.

'You're out of control, Little Fella,' she whispered. 'You have to be quiet.'

She tried to feed him as quickly as possible. He sat and fell, moved his wobbly back legs and sat again.

In the end she gave him the bowl. He shoved his whole face in, licking and snuffling wildly.

'Slow down,' she murmured and he paused to gaze up at her. Two twitches of amber in each eye, and then he was back in the bowl, hoovering up the remainder of the mush.

It was a difficult enough thing to keep a secret sleeping dragon, let alone one that was trying to sit up and snorting into bowls of Weet-Bix. Eventually he grew weary. He nudged closer to her and she scooped him up in his hoodie nest and nursed him.

'Ouch,' she said at the expanding pain in her heart.

She never, ever would have expected magic to be so painful.

And exhausting. Her eyelids grew heavy.

It's okay.

When he was finally sleeping, she placed him in the wardrobe and tiptoed to the kitchen. Her mother was there this time.

'Were you sneezing before?' she asked, not glancing up from her phone. She sounded tense. 'You could have woken him.'

'No,' said Pip. 'I wasn't sneezing.'

'I thought I heard you really sneezing,' said her mum, typing something furiously into the phone. She swore under her breath. 'Remember to take one of those pills.'

'Sure. What are you looking at?'

Ab exercises that aren't boring aromatic weight loss tea seven flavours natural rose fertilisers art classes for stress relief how to lose belly fat living the life you want to live study marine biology online nine no-fail chicken dinner recipes cute casual summer outfits be beach body ready in six weeks seven habits skinny people live by roses dying in heat can I fertilise roses in summer?

'Airfares,' she said.

'Okay,' said Pip, barely audible. Barely breathing. How would she get Little Fella on a plane?

But she knew for a fact her mum didn't have any money to buy an airfare. Matt had made her stop working at the senior's centre ages ago once she'd paid off the rest of his four-wheel drive. That was where she had taught exercise classes to older people. He said he didn't like her going around in gym clothes like that. Pip had wondered what *like that* meant. Matt said *like that* a lot. Why did you cook it *like that*? Why are you looking at me *like that*? I knew you'd say something *like that*.

She took a cup from the dish rack and filled it with water, glancing quickly at her mother's face. She'd obviously been crying.

'What are you staring at?' said her mum.

'Nothing,' said Pip. 'Where are we flying?'

'Away.' Her mother swiped clear whatever flights she was searching.

Powerful ways to stay positive how to boost your metabolism seven signs of true love install now: calmness the anxiety reduction program five foods for good moods.

'Remember what I said about the car?' said Pip, tentatively. 'We just take the car.'

Her mother hushed her, shook her head.

'What did grandma say?' Pip refused to give up.

Her mother shook her head again, mouthed, *He'll hear.*

He wouldn't, Pip knew it. He was snoring loudly. Yet her mother seemed terrified.

'My hand's better,' Pip half-lied. Anything to make her mother happy, to stop her looking so scared.

She held up her hand. She had removed the bandage in her room and found that there wasn't even a mark anymore. The deep ache was still there. It came rhythmically, building over minutes, growing and growing until it reached a crescendo before subsiding again. Each time it grew she knew something was happening to her.

A good thing, she was sure. Almost sure. She didn't feel scared any longer.

She couldn't explain that to her mother.

'Must be good antibiotics,' said her mum.

'Are you okay?' Pip asked.

'Of course,' said her mother, smiling. 'You know I'm okay.'

Pip hated that worse than any of it. Worse than the shouting, the rumbling rock words, the blaring television hiding his meanness. She hated the next day cover-ups.

Matt would wake up soon and they'd all pretend it never happened. Mum wouldn't cry. Pip wouldn't cry. Matt *definitely* wouldn't cry. Matt said 'real boys don't cry', but they did. She'd seen Mika cry and she'd liked him even more for it. The problem with most boys was that they held all their crying in and then when they did it was like Krakatoa. *Kaboom*, they blurted out their tears, all snotty and hot. They wailed and behaved as though the world was about to end over a stolen Pokémon card or coming fourth in a race or getting picked on, one too many times. If they'd let their tears out more often, they'd be okay. They wouldn't nearly destroy civilisation every time they cried.

'Can I go for a ride?' she asked.

'Where to?'

'Maybe to visit Emily,' she lied.

'Really?' said her mum, sounding shocked.

'What?'

'Nothing. Just . . . that's great,' said her mother. 'You go near that creek again, though, and I'll be so angry.'

'I promise I won't.'

She had another place in mind.

THE MORNING AFTER THE BIG STICK AND the waterhole, Mika was waiting for her at the end of her street, sitting in the gutter. He asked her how her tyre was.

'Still working,' she said.

'Told you I could fix tyres,' he said. She shrugged at that.

'How come you aren't riding it?' he asked.

She didn't want to say *because you don't have a bike.* Her cheeks burned.

They went to Erap Street, where Mika lived. His backyard ended where the banks of the creek began, steep banks, strewn with gum tree limbs that had fallen or washed there in the floods. He said at night he heard things down there below the backyard.

'What kind of things?'

'Footsteps. Sometimes trees falling. Dogs barking. Sometimes voices. Cars, far away. Fruit bats fighting. Something big moving. Now I know about your waterhole, I mean, maybe it was the bunyip. Or a werewolf.'

'Are you serious?' she asked him.

'Well, just saying,' he'd replied.

He lived in a company house with his great-grandmother, Mrs Jarvinen. He'd never met her before that night he arrived on *The Inlander*. He never even knew he had one, his own grandmother being dead. The thought hadn't occurred. 'She was a good surprise,' was how he put it. Mika was definitely a glass half-full type of boy.

The house was neat and everything had its own place. A vinyl tablecloth and a laminate bowl filled with plastic fruit. A laminate sideboard filled with Royal Doulton china. A wedding picture in an arched frame. Cushions arranged neatly on the vinyl sofa. Carefully dusted fabric flowers in plain vases. A two-seater table in the kitchen as though she'd been waiting.

Mrs Jarvinen was like her house: neat and no nonsense.

Well you are just as skinny as a bag of bones and not much else, she'd said to him when he arrived, then cooked him up mashed potato and sausages right then in the middle of the night. Mika said the smell of it was so delicious that he heard a noise and realised it was his belly.

You're not much more than an alley cat, are you?

She had given him her one good woollen blanket over a starched white sheet on the spare bed. She told him everything had a way of working out in life and that night with the train still rocking inside him and his mother, somewhere, driving across the Nullarbor Plain, he was glad he'd found her.

'You're the Gemmell girl, aren't you?' Mrs Jarvinen said when she saw Pip.

It was a simple question but sounded ominous. Maybe Mrs Jarvinen knew about the pawpaws she sometimes stole. Or the mulberries.

'Geez, don't look so guilty,' said Mika.

'I'm not,' said Pip and she'd nervously laughed, which made old Mrs Jarvinen smile. She had a deeply furrowed face and when she smiled it gave Pip the feeling it might crack into pieces.

'Well, you keep this boy in line Pippa because he's always up to something. He's cunning as a fox. Always trying to get another biscuit from the barrel without me knowing.'

Mika's room was the barest room she'd ever seen. A single bed with the grey woollen blanket. His green backpack contained his worldly possessions and he showed them to her. There was a book called *Our Universe*, which had a spaceship on the front cover. The book seemed old, like it wouldn't have the most up-to-date information on the universe but Mika touched it like it was a holy relic. 'Was my mum's when she was a kid,' he'd said. He also had a rather battered pocket Russian–English dictionary.

'Why have you got that?'

'You never know,' he replied, quite seriously.

He had some more of the *Unexplained* magazines that he shared with the other boys at school. Ghost stuff mainly. Headless people who haunted various places; schools, mostly. When Pip flipped through the pages of one, there was lots of stuff on black holes, which would explain his obsession.

'They were Mum's,' he said, watching her. 'They're really good.'

He had the tyre repair kit. And the yellow torch with his name written down one side in pen, which he'd shone into the waterhole. He flashed it on and off several times to show her it worked. Then there was the folded map of Australia, with the dotted line extending almost to Perth.

'Has she written you a letter?'

'No, that's where I reckon she'd be by now though. When she gets there, she'll be able to buy stamps.'

He gestured towards his bedroom. 'My life,' he said cheerfully.

There was a *Spider-Man* comic poster on the wall. That didn't seem right. Pip knew he would have much preferred *Doctor Who* or Sherlock Holmes, even on that second day of knowing him without *really* knowing him.

He followed her glance. 'The neighbour gave it to gran; told her I'd like it. I couldn't say no.'

'Oh.' She didn't really know what else to say.

Suddenly, she felt ridiculous sitting in a house she didn't know with a boy she didn't know. As though sensing it, he clasped his hands together and said, 'So.'

'So?' Pip replied.

'So,' he repeated. 'I think we need to look for clues.'

'Clues?'

'Bunyip clues.'

'Like footprints?'

'Yeah.'

'You're silly,' she laughed, but she liked him. The whole blue-skyed Saturday stretched out ahead of them.

'Any other places you could show me?' he asked.

She had many. Special places where termites had scribbled words all over fallen trees or haunted places where white gums stood silent like sentinels at a bend in the river. The Junction where there was a rumoured whirlpool that sucked children to their deaths. A lonely place where towering red anthills stood like tombstones. The Junkyard where people abandoned things like fridges and empty suitcases, ladders and broken wheelbarrows.

Her places. But she could share them.

'Let's go,' she said.

SATURDAY MORNING IN THE SUBURBS AND she was alone with a dragon in her backpack. The sun bleached clothes on Hills hoists and shrivelled grass. The mine blast alarms sounded and, deep beneath her feet, the earth shuddered.

Mika, she said, to the blue sky as she rode.

Today her left hand felt heavy. It was completely unmarked but it felt much heavier than the other, like it contained an invisible bowling ball. Each time the ache grew and released, some weight had been added to her, she knew it.

What do you think's happening to me?

Mika liked to come up with theories. He didn't

rush them. He said, *Let me think about that.* He lay on riverbanks, on his bed, on the concrete circle at the top of Gallipoli Park, which he believed was a landing pad for UFOs.

'I think it was where an old water tower stood,' she'd argued. She liked to debunk his theories. It was almost a pastime.

'Was,' he'd replied.

Now, she wished for a theory from him. Any theory. Mika knew things. The tallest mountain in the solar system: Olympus Mons. The depth of the Mariana Trench: almost 11,000 metres. How long it would take to travel to the nearest star: over 80,000 years. *Why is my hand aching and growing heavier?*

Silence.

Her skin felt tight too, on her left arm, as though it had shrunk a size. It wasn't painful, just weird. She opened and shut her hand as she rode.

I wish I had a friend to help me.

There, she'd thought it. There was no skirting around the issue anymore. It was a hard and lonely business saving a dragon.

She thought of her grandma, all those kilometres away, with her wild animal-saving equipment. She'd know what to do. Pip allowed herself to hope again. *We'll get there*, she hoped. *Please let us get there*, more forcefully, like a prayer. *It will happen*, she hoped as she rode to the deserted drive-in picture theatre two streets away.

It had a tall barbed wire fence reinforced with a perimeter of tangled weed and bushes. The old derelict ticket box had smashed windows. The panels in the towering screen had long ago been dismantled and all that remained was the metal frame, like some kind of giant square antenna pointed at the sky.

Pip knew exactly where the fence was broken. She dropped her bike and crawled on her hands and knees through the hole and along a short tunnel through lantana and bellyache bush, the ground littered with ring-pulls, bottle tops and straws. A fat blue-tongue slithered swiftly out of her way.

The old drive-in picture theatre was the emptiest place she'd ever been and that's why she liked it. It was a calm empty. A good empty. It was exactly the kind of empty she needed. Mika had said it freaked him out, whenever they went there, which was often. Mika liked to be freaked out. Mika said the drive-in was separated from the world somehow. 'Like when you're in here, time is moving differently. Do you feel it, Pip?' he said. 'It's definitely some kind of . . . portal.'

'I don't know,' she said. Because she didn't and that was the truth.

It was just a calm empty place and it had once been filled by lots of people and now they were all gone. Places felt strange after that happened.

Her mum had told her about the drive-in and what it was like when it was a busy place. Those acres of undulating concrete waves had been packed with cars perched like they were surfing, and the place hummed with people: kids in their pyjamas on blankets and teenagers at the kiosk and her mum and her real father kissing beneath the bright Milky Way. Pip couldn't imagine her mother being carefree enough to lie on a blanket kissing someone beneath the stars.

The place was still an acre of concrete undulating in waves, but silent now. Parts of the waves had been cracked and eroded by years of sun and there were drifts of broken concrete, fist-sized. Mika and Pip had competitions to see how far they could throw them. She'd always been much better than him.

There were also the rusted remains of the speakers that once hooked to each car door. Mika liked to pick them up and talk into them, while staring up at the skeleton of the old screen.

'Is there anyone out there?' he'd ask. 'Anyone out there?'

She picked one up now, held it in her hand before raising it to her mouth.

'Can you hear me, Mika?' she said. 'Are you there, Mika?'

The blue dome of the sky stared back at her.

Pip shook her head to dislodge those thoughts. She sat, legs folded on the crest of one of the hills, with the backpack in front of her. She searched the sky for hawks. A hawk might kill Little Fella.

When she opened the backpack he was peering up at her and she felt the great swell inside her again. Her heavy hand ached suddenly and she felt a deep pull inside it.

The little amber lightning twitches moved across his dark eyes and she knew he could see her properly.

'Hello, Little Fella,' she said, ignoring the pain in her hand and her heart. Those amber lines were beautiful; they bled into the darkness and reformed. Looking into Little Fella's eyes was like looking into a lava lamp. He sat up, quite well, drew his back legs under him, held himself upright with his front legs, and didn't wobble so much. He turned his little head to one side and gazed right back at her. He made the friendly rattling maraca noise.

Her palm ached again when he gazed at her like that. It was all connected somehow but she didn't know how.

Maybe, said Mika.

He sounded far away. Further away than he'd ever been. She held her breath.

'Maybe what?' she said.

Maybe in your hand there's . . . She could barely hear him . . . *An opening*.

'Opening?' she said but it was just the blue sky again and she was alone.

Little Fella looked at the sky and sniffed.

'Big sky, Little Fella,' Pip said. His wings, neatly folded with her sticky tape and paddle-pop sticks, had swiftly grown rigid. They stiffened as though he was about to fly.

'No way, little dude.'

She scooped him up into her lap and took out the Weet-Bix box and mixed him a bowl. He forgot the sky; his wings relaxed, and he ate a bowl in twenty seconds. His little tail lashed happily from side to side. He was puppy-sized now, having grown almost three sizes in three days and Pip felt very proud that she'd done that. She'd saved him.

'I know how to look after dragons, don't I?' she said to him, as his snout ploughed through a second bowl.

When he finished, he licked his lips with his little black tongue and gazed at her again. His eyes didn't leave hers even though she knew he was thinking of the sky. She put out her forearm towards him, instinctively, like she'd always known how to do it and he took his first two steps towards her, climbed the last step until he wobbled on her arm.

You did it, she wanted to say but she was suddenly singing instead, his flickering amber eyes fixed on hers.

The humming song, the moaning song, the weeping song.

She didn't fight it.

You did it, you're getting better, her song said in the strange singing language and she wondered what it sounded like to him. What any of it was like for him. A dragon would be used to the taste of the sky and scraping through wet clouds. Not being raised in a girl's bedroom eating mushed biscuit.

He watched her with his lava lamp eyes as she sang, and she knew he was thinking of the sky and also of what was inside her.

She didn't know how she knew, but she knew.

She knew it exactly the way a clock knows only to tick forwards.

The way apples have their seeds inside.

She knew it was a question, too.

What *was* inside her?

She was a scrawny little white girl on the outside. Plain light brown hair. Dark-eyed. Freckled. But *inside*?

'I don't know,' she said. She'd stopped singing, wiped at the tears with her free hand.

'Sad?' she asked him. His eyes reflected back the answer.

A big mountain of sad.

'Stop it.' She broke his gaze.

She didn't even have time to feel bad about that because she sensed a sudden movement beside her face. A large brown wing hit her square in the head and Little Fella was wrenched from her forearm.

'No!'

She was up fast, grabbing a concrete shard in her hand. She was all muscle, all instinct. She screamed as she hurled the shard, watched it soar and connect with the hawk's tail as it began to gain height. It was a weak strike but enough to cause the predator to flinch and drop Little Fella from its talons. Pip lunged across the concrete, scraping her knees and elbows, to land protectively over him.

'Oh no, oh no, oh no,' she cried, scanning the sky. The hawk was high above now, circling. 'Little Fella, are you okay?'

He lay quite still on the concrete.

SHE WAS PROBABLY THE MOST USELESS
dragon rescuer who ever lived. If there was a scale.
If there was a BuzzFeed list. 10 Worst Dragon Rescuers
of All Time. She'd be on there.

'I'm sorry, I'm sorry, I'm sorry, I'm sorry, I'm sorry,'
she said. No singing. Definitely no singing. The singing
link between them was severed.

He was alive in her arms, taking little shuddering
breaths. She wrapped him in the hoodie. There wasn't
a mark on him so perhaps it was shock. That's what
she hoped. She hoped it and hoped it and hoped it
like that might blast it into being. It was shock, the
way birds that fly into glass windows were sometimes

shocked, and if you warmed them up and kept them still for ten minutes, then they'd wake up and fly again.

'Please don't die,' she said. She'd only just saved him.

She grabbed her backpack and ran for the bushes to get out of the sun and away from predators. She crawled into the tunnel of lantana and rubbish and nursed him in her arms.

'Are you all right?'

He didn't open his eyes. His breathing was slowing though. More even, less jagged.

'It came from nowhere,' she said.

He curled himself abruptly into a ball, his head almost disappearing into the tight knot of himself, as though he'd had enough of her apologies.

'Okay,' she said, breathing one great shuddering breath. She was sure she hadn't breathed for the last five minutes. 'Okay.'

That movement was a good sign.

She would never, ever make a mistake like that again, having him out in the open like that. Never. She promised him and herself silently. She crouched in the shady tunnel, head in her hands, promising.

She knew she'd have to go home even though she felt like she should stay there promising all day. How could she save a dragon and then nearly kill it, seriously!

Geez, don't be so hard on yourself, Mika said, quite clearly, quite loudly, like he'd travelled the vast distance from where he'd gone, across a universe, to say those words.

'Shut up Mika,' Pip said aloud.

The sun was already high and her mother had wanted her home for lunch and her antibiotic. She looked at her skinned knees, both of them bleeding. Her elbows too.

'Let's go home, Little Fella,' she said as she lowered his tightly coiled form into her backpack and felt a sudden surge of anger, again, that she had to do this all alone. She crawled on her very sore hands and knees through the tunnel and back towards the hole in the fence.

She'd be in trouble as soon as she got home, for having bleeding knees and elbows. Trouble was her permanent state of existence. Trouble was what it felt like to be Pip. She stopped, checked on Little Fella, then zipped up the bag and crawled as fast as she could out through the hole towards her bike.

And there was Laura Denning waiting for her.

ACT II

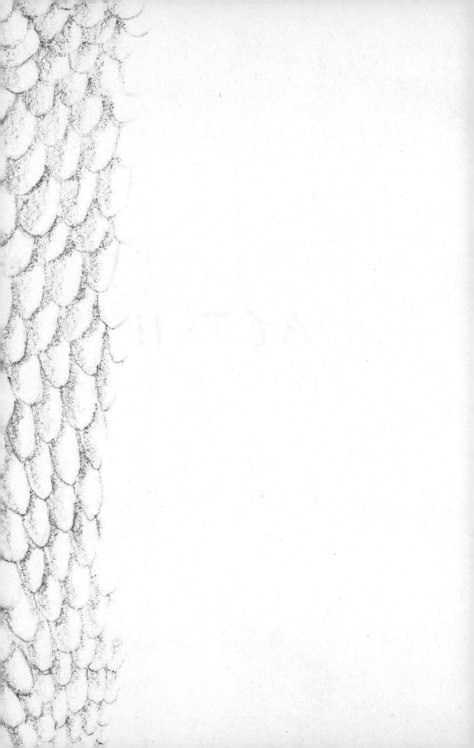

L AURA DENNING WAS STANDING THERE IN her brand-new non–light-up sneakers. She was dressed in a yellow jumpsuit covered in pink flamingos with a purple bow at her waist and a lilac satin bow in her side pony. Laura Denning was awash with bows. She was like a merry ship full-sail at sea, things fluttering and flapping. She was astride her pink bike, which had mauve tinsel streamers at the handlebars and they fluttered too.

'What are you doing here?' Pip asked.

'What were you doing in there?' replied Laura.

'How'd you know I was in there?'

'I saw you go in,' said Laura. 'I've been waiting for ages.'

'Why were you spying on me?'

'I wasn't,' said Laura and she sounded genuinely hurt. 'I just saw you crawl in there when I was riding past to Tiffany's house, so I came back to wait. My mum said never to go into the old drive-in, bad people might be in there.'

'You really should have stayed at Tiffany's,' said Pip.

'Tiffany wasn't home. She was at a gymnastics competition,' said Laura.

Pip shifted uncomfortably, one foot to the other, acutely aware of Little Fella, only freshly injured, in her backpack.

'Your knees are bleeding,' said Laura.

Pip looked down at her thongs and her dirty blood-stained kneecaps. Her bike shorts and her old T-shirt. Her brown hair tied back without any thought. Laura rustled and flapped in the hot breeze. She wanted to say something, Pip could sense it.

'I feel . . .' Laura started, then stopped. She brushed her doll-blonde fringe out of her eyes. She squinted against the noon sun. 'What was it?'

'It was nothing,' said Pip quietly. Of all the people

in the world to take an interest in what creature was inside her backpack, she never ever would have guessed it would be glitter princess Laura Denning.

All that silent wishing to not be alone and the universe had sent her *Laura Denning.*

'You shouldn't lie,' said Laura. 'You'll grow a big nose.'

'I've really got to go home,' said Pip. She picked up her pushbike and started to walk but Laura moved her bike in the way, wheel to wheel.

'Is it in your backpack now?'

'There's nothing in my backpack,' hissed Pip.

'Then why do you need a backpack?' hissed Laura.

All that hissing of words and Little Fella must have woken up. He hissed too and then rattled for good measure. It was perfectly audible. It was an I've-forgiven-you-already-I-want-Weet-Bix-mush hiss and rattle.

Pip watched Laura who was standing there with her mouth open.

'What the—' was all Laura could manage.

Quick thinking, said Mika, closely and calmly in her head.

'You would never understand,' was the best Pip could come up with.

'I'm not leaving until you explain.'

And suddenly the weight of trying to keep a small dragon alive all by herself was more than Pip could bear. She was exhausted. She'd nearly let Little Fella be killed. The universe had sent her Laura Denning.

It was inevitable. Like a tide.

Like the moon rising.

Like the sun going down.

'Come home with me,' she shrugged. 'I'll show you in my bedroom.'

'Okay,' said Laura. She looked kind of shocked at how easy it had been.

'You have to promise me you won't tell a soul.'

'I promise,' said Laura Denning.

'**P**ROMISE ME, YOU'LL ALWAYS TAKE YOUR feet out at night,' Mika had said. 'That's when bunyips come out.'

He'd read it in a book, he said.

'I don't think there is a bunyip,' Pip said. 'No offense.'

He was unfazed by her lack of belief.

'See?' said Mika at the river, the second time they went to the waterhole. 'These could be bunyip footprints.'

'Or they could belong to a wallaby?' suggested Pip.

She'd seen wallabies there. Plenty of them. Also cows that had escaped from their barbed wire fences on the hill side of town. A skittish lone horse once, trotting down the middle of the baked dry riverbed. Kookaburras. Goannas. Cranky frillneck lizards that refused to back away. Hawks, endlessly circling above in the sky. Snakes. A brown snake had crossed the bulldust road in front of her feet once and disappeared just as swiftly into the dry grass, minding its own business.

She told Mika that story.

'You could have been a goner,' he said.

He wanted to know everything. How close the snake was to her feet. What type of brown it was. Its length. Mika was like that with stories. He was greedy for them. He absorbed them. He sucked them from books and television and news broadcasts. He absorbed them from movies. He drew them out of people constantly. He knew the story of Laura and her concussion when she fell from a pony at pony club. He knew she saw double for two days. That there were two fish in the hospital goldfish bowl when she first opened her eyes but really there was only one. He'd extracted that from Laura even though Laura didn't particularly like him in those early days. He knew Mrs Green in Admin was a twin and that her twin was exactly like her only she lived on the other side of the world and that if Mrs Green got a headache, her twin sister got a headache at exactly the same time.

As far as Pip could remember she'd never even seen Mika talk to Mrs Green.

'What if Mrs Green's twin is like an evil twin?' said Mika.

'Or what if Mrs Green is the evil twin and her sister is the good one?' countered Pip.

Mika's eyes widened with delight in the way that made Pip laugh.

Mika slurped up stories and now he was trying to slurp the snake story out of Pip. Pip wasn't used to talking like that. She liked to blend into the background, not step forwards and tell tales; except he was so interested.

It felt like forever since someone had listened to her.

Matt had only recently moved in but Pip's mum had been seeing him for months before. He sent her one million text messages a day. The phone *ping*, *ping*, *ping*, *ping*ed and all those messages affected her mum's hearing. Pip tried to tell her things. Things that happened at school. Things that she saw on the way home. Things she heard on the news. 'Really?' her mum would say, pretending to listen as she replied to Matt's texts.

Mika gobbled up Pip's snake story and smiled. He told her one about a snake that ate a man in Malaysia, which led to a story about an elephant that trampled people in a village in India, which somehow led to a story about a whole town that drowned when a molasses factory exploded.

They pretended to look for bunyip tracks although really, they were just feasting on each other's stories. She didn't have stories like his, but she told him about how she picked the Melbourne Cup winner for her mum three years in row until her streak ran out. How once a long time ago her mum told her that if a butterfly flapped its wings in South America it could cause a cyclone in Australia, although she couldn't really remember how. How she had a dream once that a UFO landed at primary school and that they all hid in the toilet block with their feet up on the toilet seats but some of the kids were taken away.

'Like which kids?'

'Laura Denning,' said Pip, giggling.

'And then they gave her straight back seconds later,' Mika said and cacked himself over that.

He was patient with her stories, which were a bit slippery. She stumbled over some of them. She got mixed up with the story of her grandfather who was in the war, because she couldn't quite remember which war it was. Mika suggested wars. He said, 'I bet it was Vietnam.'

She showed him the junkyard, and the haunted trees at the river bend. They walked halfway to the junction then turned back again. They ended up at the waterhole, as they always would, with the sun just setting.

'Did you know that there are at least one hundred billion stars in our galaxy?' he said, lying on his belly, drawing the spiral in the dark water.

She did know. He'd told her twice already. Plus, there was a black hole in the middle, called Sagittarius A.

'Hey, you never told me what you needed the getaway tunnel for,' she replied.

She wanted to hear a story about him. Apart from the survivor on a train story, his tales were all about other things, other people, other places, other happenings – black holes, not him.

He had leaned forwards though, staring in the water where the darkening blue sky was held, for the first time not paying her attention.

'I really wish I knew how deep this was,' he said.

They rode their bikes the two streets in silence, Pip arguing loudly with herself the whole way. She was having second thoughts. This would go bad, real bad. Laura would probably scream. She was a screaming, squealing type of girl. She'd scream and then she'd run all the way to her house and tell her mother who would ring the police. She'd squeal and there'd be sirens. Laura Denning wasn't the type of girl who could keep secrets.

It'll be okay, said Mika.

No, it won't, said Pip.

You can't do it alone, he replied.

Pip held open her front gate for Laura and showed her where to rest her bike.

'How's your hand?' asked Laura.

Pip looked at her left hand, perfectly healed but heavy as a small planet. Where something was *opening*, she knew it, like a black hole.

Yes, she couldn't do it by herself anymore. It was inevitable.

She's better than no one, said Mika.

'My hand,' said Pip, staring at it. 'It's getting better.'

'My mum got a special cream on the internet that heals everything in one minute,' said Laura.

That was the kind of girl she was.

She was a look-at-my-braid-my-mother-watched-a-YouTube-video-on-how-to-do-it-it-took-her-nearly-an-hour type of girl. She was a just-stand-there-while-I-perform-a-Beyoncé-song-for-you girl. She was a hey-everyone-I've-got-melting-moment-biscuits-in-my-lunch-box-because-I'm-so-awesome type of girl.

Then Pip smelled something else in Laura's voice. Smelling an emotion was so weird she stopped pushing her bike and stood there. Laura's words smelled tangy, like crushed dandelions. Her words smelled nervous.

She wished that hadn't happened. That was weirder than the heart inflations and the black hole in her hand and the crying and her skin on her left arm that was one size too tight and felt like it was going to crack if it got any tighter, all rolled into one. She really didn't want to smell Laura Denning's words.

'I could get you some,' said Laura, releasing another cloud of tangy nervous words.

'It actually might come in handy,' said Pip.

Her mother had a good scolding ready and waiting, especially when she saw Pip's bloody knees, but when she saw Laura she tucked it away.

'Hi,' she said. 'It's Laura, isn't it?'

'Hi Mrs Gemmell,' said Laura.

Her mother was thinking all her Christmases had come at once. *A girl like Laura in our house. Some of it might rub off on Pip.* Pip could read all that on her mother's face in a nanosecond. She was in the kitchen cleaning, the way she cleaned sometimes, scrubbing away at the surface of things as though it might change their house. As though there might be a new one folded away beneath, a bigger one, an airier one, where everyone was relaxed and smiling and never scared.

Matt was in the kitchen too. He was freshly showered and normal-looking. Like all the shouting and stamping had never happened the night before. Pip knew all his weather patterns. Today was sunshine. Her mum was basking in its glow like a sunbaker but that would change. Pip's heart sank, her hopes withering. Then she steeled herself, refusing to give up. He might seem normal but there was more to come. He'd make her mum feel good today and bad tomorrow.

They would get to Townsville, she knew it. They had to. She could feel it.

'G'day,' Matt said, glancing up from his phone for a second.

'We're going to play something in my room,' said Pip.

'What on earth did you do to your knees?' asked her mum.

'Stacked it on my bike,' said Pip. 'Didn't I, Laura?'

Laura seemed confused. *It's the first of many lies, Laura, you better get used to it,* thought Pip.

'Yeah, big-time,' said Laura, recovering herself.

'Well clean them up with a washcloth before you play,' said Mum, coming closer. 'It's just gravel rash, right?'

Pip was aware of Little Fella shifting in her backpack.

'I'll wash them,' she said quickly and she bundled Laura down the hallway. 'We're going to be shutting the door.'

'Secret women's business?' said her mum.

'Something like that.'

She washed her knees with lightning-speed, and threw the washcloth in the dirty clothes basket.

'Quickly,' she whispered to Laura. 'He's waking up.'

Laura's eyes widened at that.

They sat on the bed, the backpack between them, Laura looking around, everywhere but at the backpack. Pip could only imagine what Laura's room was like. It would be a complete advertisement for pinks and purples, probably. Nothing like hers.

'Ouch,' Pip muttered as the skin on her left arm tightened suddenly and her hand grew heavy. The stench of Laura's anxiety was overpowering.

'Calm down,' Pip said quietly to Laura.

'I'm calm,' lied Laura.

'Do you really want to know?' she asked Laura, over the ache. 'I mean, once you know you can't unknow it. Maybe you'll have to run away with me too.'

'Run away?' Laura whispered it. There were probably kids that didn't fantasise about running away, Pip realised right then.

'Because that's probably what's going to happen,' she explained.

'Show me,' said Laura. She didn't do drama as well as Pip thought she would. Pip leaned forwards, Laura too. She began to unzip the backpack. She unzipped it slowly so she didn't give Little Fella a fright. She hoped he'd gone back to sleep, that the movement in the kitchen was him shifting in his dreams.

Those amber lightning eyes would be way too much for Laura.

Please be asleep, please be asleep.

He wasn't asleep. His head popped out of the backpack straightaway, as soon as he could push past the opening in the zipper. There was a golden storm raging in his eyes that seemed to have grown since the incident with the hawk.

He looked at Pip and then at Laura. The papery bristles on his back rustled slightly. He made a not-so-happy hiss-rattle.

And then Laura screamed.

LAURA DENNING WAS BACKWARDS OFF THAT bed, knocking over a washing basket filled with clothes, hands over her mouth, clamping in the residue of the scream.

'Oh my god,' she said in a high-pitched voice, then quieter, 'oh my god. Oh my god.'

Even though Little Fella wasn't doing anything, just staring up at them. He didn't seem like he was about to attack her.

'It's okay,' Pip said. 'He won't hurt you.'

But she thought of her hand immediately, the burning that spread through her body and turned her into a lighthouse, the stiffening of her skin, the new-found ability to smell words.

'He won't hurt,' she said again, placed a finger on her lips and motioned for Laura to be quieter.

'Oh my god,' was all Laura could whisper.

'Everything okay down there?' called Mum. 'What are you two up to?'

'Nothing, all good,' Pip yelled back.

She grabbed the Weet-Bix box off the bed and started to mush.

'Pippa?' said her mum. The stern use of her name. Pippa, the question? Pippa, you *must* be doing something wrong.

Pip went to the door and opened it a crack.

'Sorry,' she said. 'We were just playing a game.'

Little Fella could smell the mush and he was rattling and hissing and trying to get out of the backpack. Laura shuddered

'Calm down, Little Fella,' said Pip, lifting him out and then holding the Weet-Bix bowl so he didn't knock it over as he went to work slurping down the contents. 'Seriously Laura, he won't hurt you. He's tiny. Tiny as a baby puppy.'

Laura took a step closer, then two steps back when Little Fella turned, aware of movement behind him. Pip lifted him, turned him so that he was in her lap, the bowl in front of him so he could see Laura clearly.

She felt protective of him, motherly, and that inflating pain ballooned inside her chest and the tears welled in her eyes. She wiped at them because she didn't want Laura to see, there was no stopping them though, the tears dripped as she mushed another bowl. Laura watched Pip as though she were making a potion, not Weet-Bix, her mouth slightly open, the ribbon wilted in her hair. The tears didn't seem to register with her.

Laura twitched each time Little Fella moved. When he stood on all four legs to move towards the bowl, Laura jumped involuntarily.

'You're walking, Little Fella,' cried Pip. 'His name is Little Fella.'

'It's a bat, right?' whispered Laura. Her first words.

'It's not a bat,' said Pip.

'Are you sure it's not a bat?'

'It's not a bloody bat,' said Pip, wiping away the tears with one hand while holding the bowl for ravenous Little Fella. 'You're not a bat, are you, Little Fella?'

'Maybe a species of bat no one has ever seen.'

Pip could sense there was a lot of energy inside Laura. The room was cloudy with her fear. Laura was coiled tight, like she might explode any moment and run out of the room, exactly the way Pip had imagined. Her scent was not so much crushed dandelions as a whole field of them trampled. Pip knew she wanted to grab her bike and ride through the streets screaming, 'She's got a dragon!' But she was trying not to. She was trying really hard to keep her feet on the ground. She was trying not to be the running-away type, Laura Denning. Pip had to admit she felt kind of proud of her. It wasn't easy to see a dragon.

'Sit on the bed,' Pip said. 'He's a dragon. You know he is.'

'I don't know what he is,' whispered Laura as she sat on the end of the bed as far away as possible. Little Fella, snuffling and slurping, paused when he felt her weight on the bed. His paddle-popped wings bristled.

'See, he likes you,' said Pip. 'A terrible thing

happened at the old drive-in. He nearly got taken by a big hawk. It had him completely in its claws and was about to carry him away. He doesn't seem hurt though. I saved him from nearly dying, in the beginning. I found him nearly dead. It's been four days.'

Laura had no words. She sat there staring.

Little Fella gobbled, his belly growing round. He looked up, shifted his golden lava lamp gaze to Laura, and rattled happily.

'See?' said Pip. 'He's just a dragon.'

If you find a dragon you need a friend. It sounded like that could be a real saying that was in an old book somewhere. Pip had been so lonely for those four days even though she had Little Fella. Even though he'd scratched her and he was part of her and she was part of him. Even though the world was different for finding him. Everything. Her body. Her heavy hand and the tight skin on her arm and her heart. All of that and still she'd been so lonely and now she had Laura sitting on the edge of her bed.

She taught Laura how to feed him, mush the Weet-Bix, hold the bowl. He wobbled towards Laura, tentative, then gobbled just as enthusiastically. Pip felt Laura relax. She started to ask questions. Slowly at first. *Why does he eat Weet-Bix? Is that all he can eat?*

Then those questions grew in momentum. *Where did you find him? What are you going to do with him? How do you know it's a him? Why have you got paddle-pop sticks on his wings?*

How have you kept him secret from your mum? How big do you think he'll get? Where does he come from? Why were you crying?

So, she had noticed it.

'I can't help it,' said Pip. 'It happens sometimes when I hold him or look at him.'

'And that noise too?'

'What noise?'

'That low mumbly thing you were doing.'

She hadn't even realised she was doing it.

'It just happens,' she said.

Little Fella grew weary. He wobbled back to Pip and sat back in the hoodie nest on her lap. When they heard her mother's footsteps she quickly took him and placed him inside the wardrobe, threw a pillow over the Weet-Bix stuff.

Her mother knocked.

'We've got to drop Matt at cricket,' she said. 'Laura will have to go home.'

'Can't we both stay here?'

Her mum opened the door a crack.

'You know you can't, Pip,' smiled her mum. 'What are you two up to anyway? You both look suspicious.'

'Nothing,' said Pip. 'Secret girl's business.'

Pip knew her mum loved it. She would be thinking *she's normal after all. No more lost boys. No more running wild at the creek.*

They listened to her footsteps back down the hallway to the kitchen and then opened the wardrobe door. Little Fella peered up at them sleepily.

'You have to promise again,' whispered Pip. 'You can't tell anyone. Not a soul.'

'Not a soul,' said Laura. 'I promise.'

'**N**OT A SOUL' WAS SUCH A STRANGE PHRASE. Pip repeated it in her head after Laura was gone and her room felt strangely empty without her there.

Not a soul. Not a soul. Not a soul.

Soul a not. Soul a not. Soul a not.

Ton a lous. Ton a lous. Ton a lous.

She thought of Mika's soul. Souls were wispy, flappy, scraps of things. Bodies were what were needed. For all the talk of what was inside you being the most important thing, souls just drifted away without hands and toes and brains and hearts.

After Laura left, Pip checked on Little Fella sleeping in his nest, then walked out to the kitchen. Matt was picking up his phone and wallet. Her mother was hurriedly grabbing her handbag.

'She's Rob's kid,' said Matt on the way to the car. 'Isn't she?'

'Yeah, I think so,' said Mum.

'Pretty little thing,' he said. 'Rob's a loser but his wife, now *she's* hot.'

She. Thing. Pretty. Hot. Pip's mother ignored it. Pip said, 'Her name's Laura.'

Matt ignored her.

He smelled of Lynx aftershave and last night's booze. A bad smell, sweet and sour. Her mother sitting beside him smelled of worry.

Her name's Laura, she said to herself again. And Laura would be going home to her house and Saturday afternoon in Laura's house would be very different to Pip's house. In Laura's house, Laura's *Hot* Mum would be cooking something amazing for dinner, something from a recipe book. Her dad, *the loser*, would have finished making something with wood, like a birdfeeder, that little pretty sparrows would come and feed from. Everyone would be smiling at each other like in an advertisement for ice cream. They would probably all be going to watch a family-friendly movie.

Only Laura would be changed now.

She'd fed a dragon and there was no stepping back from that.

She'd be changed and fitting into her perfect life would be almost impossible. Pip smiled in the car, thinking of how Laura had been ruined. It wasn't malicious. She had been ruined in a good way. The best possible way.

Matt kissed her mother goodbye at the sports ground parking lot. It was a quick kiss but Pip knew that would keep her mother happy for hours: a tiny kiss, a little crumb, he loved her, he hadn't meant any of the angry rumbling rock words he'd thrown at her last night . . .

'Don't you prang this beauty,' he said, of his beloved black four-wheel drive, leaning in through the window and kissing her mum again.

They didn't speak much on the way home because Pip could tell her mum was savouring that, imagining things from the kiss that weren't real, like an entirely different life and a better house and a beach holiday where they were in love and no one was afraid. He'd let her drive the car too, which meant he trusted her; things were changing for the better.

'You okay?' asked Mum, absent-mindedly.

Past the mine they went, the smelter, the workshops. Past street after street of little houses like theirs.

'I'm okay,' said Pip.

'Nice of that Denning girl to come over.'

'Nice.'

'You've been so lonely since . . .'

'Mika,' said Pip. 'Yeah.'

'You used to have lots of friends, remember? Emily, Audrey . . .'

'They weren't the same,' she said, then added softly, 'We have the car.'

They could grab some clothes and throw them in a suitcase. She'd take Little Fella from the wardrobe. They could drive and drive and drive all through the afternoon and night and Townsville was at the end of that highway, shining bright.

'Don't,' said her mum, just as quietly.

Pip hoped that Little Fella was still asleep at home. She had a sudden mental image of him awake and banging his way out of the wardrobe, opening his paddle-popped wings and buzzing around the house, crashing and smashing into things. There he was though, curled in his hoodie nest when she returned. He continued to sleep for hours that afternoon. Pip went to and from the wardrobe checking on him, yet still he slept on. 'Are you okay?' she whispered, touching him gently on the back but he only stretched and then curled himself tight again, perfectly contented.

She went and lay beside her mother on her bed. There was that anxious waiting feeling in the house that happened on Saturday afternoons. Even with the kiss, it was still there. Even if something amazing happened, like the Queen came to visit, and they served her tea and fairy cakes, the waiting would be there, below the surface, like a dangerous rip. Even finding a dragon, the most miraculous thing in the world, and there was still that waiting. Matt ruined everything.

'What are you looking at?' asked Pip. Her mother was staring into her phone.

Super-foods how to shed ten kilos fast look ten years younger with this simple trick how to have a perfect hair day every day six easy at-home bad breath remedies perfect body workout how to stop roses turning brown.

'Rose fertilisers,' said her mother. 'Did you see the leaves today? They are so much greener. All I need is to find the right thing to boost them along. How's that hand of yours?'

Pip offered her hand and her mother held it, looked at it like she was going to read her palm. Pip wished she could tell her.

'What should we have for dinner?' her mum asked.

'Vanilla ice cream,' said Pip.

And that made her mother laugh.

VANILLA HAD BEEN THE NAME THAT SHE chose for the kitten they'd saved, but Mika had disagreed. They'd known each other months by that time, and it was their first and only *almost* argument.

'How could you not call it Vanilla?' she'd said. 'She's white.'

'I don't know,' he'd replied, apologetic, 'it just doesn't seem to fit her.'

Vanilla was tiny, flea-ridden and abandoned. One eye was swollen shut. She stood there simultaneously hissing and purring. Mrs Jarvinen had shuddered because she liked things neat and tidy. Mika loved that kitten, though, in a single-minded ferocious way.

He begged for kitten milk from the supermarket and he begged for it in a way that Pip had never heard him speak before. How could Mrs Jarvinen refuse him, cradling that tiny, helpless thing?

He held her while she slept.

He fed her lovingly whenever she woke with the food Mrs Jarvinen bought.

Before he went to school, he wrote down a feeding schedule for his great-grandmother. Mrs Jarvinen huffed about it but, Pip was almost certain, she wouldn't have disobeyed his orders on that kitten.

And Pip knew it was *his* kitten, not hers, although sometimes she had to point out that she was the one who actually spotted it. They would have walked right past that drain if not for her.

'I know, I know,' Mika said. 'A percentage of her belongs to you.'

'How much percentage?' she asked.

They drew up an agreement. The kitten was seventy-seven per cent his and twenty-three per cent hers. Her percentage involved being allowed to hold and feed the kitten when she was at the house, and recognition for finding it.

But really, she knew, the kitten was all his and he needed every single per cent.

'She needs a good name, Pip,' said Mika. 'Something strong. Because she's a survivor. Vanilla's not strong.'

'Maybe . . . Warrior?' said Pip.

'I like that,' he said but he kept thinking. He took *Our Universe* from his green backpack. Pip had seen him take out that book one hundred times since she'd met him. It was his talisman.

He flipped through the pages.

'Strong,' he whispered. 'Andromeda.'

'Eww,' she said.

'True,' he said. 'Virgo?'

'Nah.'

'Cygnus?'

'Never.'

'Betelgeuse?'

'Are you kidding me?'

In his Russian–English dictionary, he found the

words for 'strong' and 'cat'. 'Sil-ny kosh-ka,' he read slowly.

Pip sighed deeply.

The folded map of Australia had fallen from his backpack when he'd extracted the dictionary. Pip unfolded it and gasped. The dotted line had left Perth again and was snaking its way across the red centre.

'Is your mum coming?!'

Mika looked up from a book on the night sky that he'd borrowed from the town library.

'Maybe,' he said. 'I don't know. That's what I feel. I close my eyes and draw the dots now.'

'Oh,' said Pip.

'What about GR8 DDO 185? Like Great?' he laughed at that. 'It's a star.'

Pip rolled her eyes but she felt sad about Mika's mum. How she never called or said when she was coming.

'Hercules? Perseus? Wolf?' he said. 'Wolf?'

They gazed at the tiny kitten with the spindly legs.

'How about Ursa?' he said. 'It means "bear". You know. Like Ursa Minor and Ursa Major.'

The little kitten made a noise. It wasn't really a meow. More a *meep*.

'I like Ursa,' said Pip. 'And I think Ursa does too.'

It seemed right. The way names sometimes fit when others won't stick.

'Ursa,' said Mika, scooping the tiny bag of bones up carefully and smiling. 'Big as a bear.'

'Big as a galaxy,' said Pip.

And she knew that's how big Mika's love for that kitten was.

L OVE. THAT'S WHAT YOU NEEDED MOSTLY, TO
save things. And Weet-Bix. And spaghetti. It was a
seven Weet-Bix and one tin of spaghetti night. Little
Fella slept in small snatches although mostly he was
frisky. He'd been growing stronger and bigger all those
hours he'd been asleep. He was sturdy on his legs: he
trotted on the spot, bumped against her face while
she tried to sleep, breathing his spaghetti and Weet-
Bix breath all over her. He rolled on his back beside
her and his lava lamp eyes shimmered playfully in the
dark. His paddle-popped and sticky-taped wings made
a crinkly sound. She tickled his tummy tentatively and
he seemed to like it.

The ache still came and went in her left hand except it was less now. The ghost of an ache. She didn't shiver or burn anymore but her hand remained heavy and the tightness of her skin extended across her chest and down both thighs. She sat up and stared at her arm, held it to the night-light to check there weren't scales. Her arm looked just like her arm. Or was it brighter? Was her skin slightly brighter on her left arm? A faint glow.

She shook her head. She was imagining things.

What do you think? she asked Mika in the dark and was surprised that he was right there, close to her.

Maybe don't think, Pip, he said.

What does that mean? Do you still think it's an opening?

He didn't reply for ages. Like he was thinking about it, the way Mika always did. She was almost asleep.

Some things you can't think, he said at last.

She slept when Little Fella slept, which wasn't often. She heard Matt come home, the sound of him stumbling down the hallway and into bed. His voice was thick and rumbling and Pip tensed, waiting, but nothing happened. She realised that Little Fella was paused too, listening.

'It's okay,' she said quietly, rubbing him along his snout, around the tiny little horn nubs.

Pip woke to the sound of his belly gurgling again and she carried him quickly down the hall and towards the back door. The house was still and she was careful to not let the screen door bang. She tiptoed down the back ramp to her mother's rose garden and placed him gently on the soil just in time. He looked at her, almost embarrassed, as he began, so she glanced away, up at the clean morning sky. She held her nose this time. Dragon poo stank. The neighbour's dog growled then whimpered.

'Geez, Little Fella,' she said, shaking her head before noticing that her mum was right, there were new green shoots all over the bushes and several buds as well.

She picked him up and took him back up the ramp only to hear someone in the kitchen, the sound of the fridge door opening and then the tap running. That was a problem. A real dragon-sized problem. Pip tucked Little Fella up her pyjama shirt, his dark scales rough against her skin. She hoped he wouldn't scratch her. She untied her ponytail, held him in place with her arms across her chest and rushed through the kitchen as quickly as she could, behind her mother, who had her back turned to her at the kettle.

'Hey,' said her mum, as she passed, almost running. 'What are you doing out there at this time of the morning?'

'Needed to look at the sky,' said Pip, hightailing it down the hall. She placed Little Fella in the wardrobe; shut the door on his large, golden, not-at-all sleepy eyes. She went back to the kitchen where her mother was stirring coffee, waiting. 'Did you just bring an animal inside? What's that smell?' her mother asked.

'An animal? Huh?' said Pip. Mock confused. 'What smell?'

Was the 'huh' too much? She needed to stay calm and stay cool.

She opened the pantry cupboard and started searching for more cereal.

'Why would I have an animal?' she muttered under her breath.

Her mother sighed. Sniffed the air. 'It's fading. Sorry, must be imagining things.'

'Must be,' said Pip, pouring cornflakes. Would he eat cornflakes? When her mother went to sit on the front steps with her phone, she'd have to fill a container for later, just in case. But her mother didn't go. She stood there sipping her coffee. Pip thought she could hear Little Fella bump once against the wardrobe so she talked loudly to cover it.

'I wanted to look at the sky to see if there was a moon because . . . it was so bright last night.'

'Shhh, you'll wake him up,' said her mum, staring down at her phone.

Best body exfoliator perfect nails at home pedicure seven-minute body workouts that don't need a gym does my phone have spyware on it university for mature-age students download enrolment forms scuba diving for beginners best reefs to snorkel in Australia Townsville best primary schools women's helpline how to turn off location tracking on your phone.

In Townsville they'd never have to whisper. They'd never have to feel scared. Her mother's face would be relaxed again; she'd smile her old smile and laugh her old laugh. She'd know about Little Fella too. They'd raise him together until they could get him back to where he belonged. While they were raising him, Matt would become a memory; he'd fade away and become flimsy and inconsequential, little more than a scrap of paper. They'd crumple him up and throw him away.

Her mother raised her eyes from the phone and stared at Pip, as though she was going to say something. Something really important.

Maybe: *I know you have a dragon.*

Maybe: *Let's run away, Pip. I know I've said it before, but I really want to now. You're right, we'll take the car. We'll go while he's at work.*

Maybe—

There was a knock at the door.

'Bit early in the morning on a Sunday,' said her mum.

Pip was frozen. What if it were the authorities? Maybe Laura Denning told her mother and her mother has phoned the council stray animals department. Or the police.

If it was the police she'd have to run fast. That was one thing she was good at; she won all her races at school. She'd run to the wardrobe. Dragon into backpack. Down the back stairs, over the back fence.

'Quick, before it wakes Matt,' hissed Mum.

'Okay, okay,' whispered Pip. She took a breath and opened the front door.

IT WAS ONLY LAURA.

'Hi Laura,' said Mum, smiling. 'You're early.'

'Couldn't sleep,' said Laura with a weak smile. She was pale, worried-looking although her hair was elaborately braided. She was wearing a yellow shirt festooned with glitter love hearts and the words 'I BELIEVE IN UNICORNS' but her face was different; there were dark crescents beneath her eyes.

'Have you told someone?' said Pip, when they were in her bedroom.

'No,' said Laura. 'I've just been thinking. All night.'

Pip couldn't smell Laura today. That sudden and strange power seemed to have evaporated. She could still sense that something was wrong though. Pip opened the wardrobe door and Little Fella was waiting for them, golden-eyed. Laura made a noise, a sigh, an almost moan.

'Come on, Little Fella,' Pip said, scooping him up in the hoodie nest. She sat on the bed and Laura began to mush Weet-Bix without even being asked. The worried look faded a little on her face. Little Fella gobbled and gulped down two bowls in quick succession.

'I brought this,' said Laura, taking a little pink blanket, a doll's blanket, from her mauve backpack.

'Thanks,' said Pip, trying to hide her disdain.

Through Laura's left braid there was a purple ribbon threaded. Beneath the yellow 'I BELIEVE IN UNICORNS' T-shirt, there was a white denim skirt and to complete the outfit she was wearing glitter flats. It was totally impractical dress for dragon care. But Pip noticed something else about her. She had some words on her tongue and she wasn't saying them.

'Spit it out,' said Pip.

The worried expression returned to Laura's face.

Worried was not a normal expression for Laura. Laura could look pouty, petulant at times, if she didn't get her own way at school, through to supremely self-confident, self-assured and smug.

'Um,' said Laura and her face crumpled a little before she quickly composed herself.

'I did warn you,' said Pip, feeling her way around Laura's unsaid words. 'I mean, you can't not know it once you know it.'

'It's not that,' said Laura, quickly. Tears welled in her blue eyes. She blinked them away. Softer, 'It's not that.'

'What then?'

'It's just . . . I keep thinking. I keep feeling.'

'Feeling what?'

'A *song*.'

She said it so powerfully that some of those tears shook loose and a little snot too from her nose. She made a noise, like she was going to wail or cry, but she did neither. Her face flushed and a storm of blotches appeared with the effort of her trying to stop the tears.

Pip was surprised by how strong Laura actually was, fighting the urge of that song.

And to tell the truth, she was jealous. Because she thought it was only her with the singing. She thought it was Little Fella's connection with *her*. Apparently, he made anyone who came in contact with him want to sing those songs that they'd forgotten about. It wasn't a burning jealousy; she let it go as quickly as it came. She felt a sudden wave of pity for Laura who was fighting it and then she returned to begrudging admiration.

'Laura,' she said.

Laura was staring at the window, intent on ignoring Little Fella, who was looking backwards and forwards between them, waiting for his Weet-Bix.

'What?'

'You shouldn't fight it.'

A sob then. A real big gulpy snotty sob.

Because poor Laura never knew anything but stuff: purple ribbons and hula hoops and apps that dressed up kittens and pony club and light-up sneakers and squishy makeovers on YouTube and how to make pink glitter slime and now, *now*, she had a forgotten song inside her that was dark and deep and she was looking at a dragon with golden eyes.

When Laura sang it was different. It was like Laura was a true dragon singer. *That's the only title for it*, Pip thought: *a True Dragon Singer*. If there were any small crumbs of jealousy leftover, they were blown away with leaf blower force, because Laura's singing was meant to be. Laura sang the truth.

Her first note was long and beautiful and she seemed so shocked by it that tears just fell out of her eyes. The shock passed quickly though, because there was another note coming from deeper down and she needed to let it come up to the surface. Laura's song was sweet and sad. It wasn't growly and guttural and full of gritty hums like Pip's. Laura's notes were clear. You could almost hear the sky in them. Other places. The tilting earth.

Little Fella, his belly full of Weet-Bix, gazed at Laura. He shuddered slightly, a yes, and climbed into Pip's lap. Laura wiggled forwards, so that their knees were touching, still singing. Pip could smell her up close like that; a toothpaste and clean clothes smell but her song-words, they were different. They were made of stone and steep places and storms.

Laura touched Little Fella. She hovered her hands over him. She touched his dark scales, the tufts of papery stuff on his back, and then her attention turned to his paddle-popped and sticky-taped wings. She folded out one wing gently and sang. Her notes undulated, up and down, like the wind.

Pip cried. Or at least she must have because when Laura had finished and the song had dried up, the way those songs did, her cheeks were wet.

'You're good at that,' said Pip, after a while.

Little Fella was asleep in her lap. His wings looked the same but Pip knew they were stronger. 'Good' wasn't the right word though, she knew that, even as she said it. She shrugged, shook her head. Kids were 'good' at drawing and weaving friendship bracelets and running cross-country. This couldn't be more different. Laura seemed much calmer now. Her eyes were puffy from crying but she smiled.

'You know what I mean,' Pip said. 'You're a proper Dragon Singer or something.'

'Yeah,' Laura said, accepting that role without any of her usual boastfulness.

They sat there quietly watching him. Matt still slept. Pip's mother drank coffee in the sunshine staring at the green shoots on her roses. Mika was silent in her head, like he knew this wasn't his place to say anything.

Like he knew Pip had a friend in this.

A real live friend.

A friend who could help her save that dragon and send it home.

Pip's hand ached suddenly, a new sharp ache, and her skin tightened from her fingertips to her shoulder and then across her chest.

'You know,' said Pip, softly and so very sadly, 'we can't keep him forever.'

'I KNOW A HILL,' SHE'D TOLD MIKA AFTER
those first few months, almost like she was talking
about an old friend. Of all her places it was the hardest
for her to share so she'd saved it to last.

There was a road that ran right past her hill. It led
to the cemetery and the dump. When she stepped off
that road and threw her bike into the gully though, she
always felt far away from anywhere. And, in a way that
she couldn't explain in words, she always felt that hill
was waiting for her.

It was hummock grass and spinifex spotted, filled
with spiny crooked places. Parts of that hill leaned

at unnatural angles; it folded in on itself in pleats. It provided ledges on the desert side for viewing the vastness of things and ledges on the town side for viewing the huge dark mine, the smelters and stacks gushing sulphur fumes up into the cloudless blue sky. It offered up worn paths that led to nowhere but sheer drops.

When she thought she'd explored it all, she'd find something else: a stand of jagged edged stone, folded into the mountain's side; a silver tree, its heart eaten out and replaced with a chamber of termites' scribblings; a tiny blood-red sapling trying to grow itself out of a crack in a rock.

Yet all that time it had kept the cave a secret from her.

Kept it for the right time. Until Mika was there.

They discovered it after days of exploring and doing dangerous things. Things she wouldn't have done without a partner. Picking their way down into the pleats and crouching in the dark, shaded spaces before climbing back out again. The cave was there waiting on the desert side beneath a path that led to the side of the hill. Mika lay down and she'd held his legs so he could shuffle forwards as far as possible to see what was below.

'There's rock but it's got good foot places, apart from this first bit. There's a ledge down there.'

'How far down?'

'A couple of metres.'

A couple of metres didn't seem much. Not on that hill with the huge blue dome of the sky above them. She'd gone over first, because she was good at rock climbing. She said it and Mika didn't disagree because he wasn't the sort of boy who thought boys were better at everything than girls. He stayed on his belly, ready to give her his hand if she got stuck.

It was true the hill gave no help for the first part. It deliberately wanted to keep that ledge hidden. She climbed backwards over the edge and had to stretch her leg a long way down to find the first place for her foot, but once her foot was there, it was easier. Mika's hand grew farther away. It was a reckless idea. One slip. One fall in the wrong direction and there was nothing . . .

It was terrifyingly exciting.

She could see the ledge now and the cave that had been hidden by the overhang.

'There's a cave!' she cried before jumping the last metre to the ground.

It took longer for Mika, that first time, but she coaxed him.

'To the right,' she said, of the first stage, 'and reach down.'

'I'm not Mr Stretch,' he said, laughing nervously and his laughing made her laugh, him hanging there like that, gripping onto nothing but stone.

'You *have* to stretch,' she said.

When he'd jumped the last metre, they'd both stood there mesmerised by the place. They crept in under the rock overhang and touched their hands to the ceiling. Sat on the packed earth floor, barely breathing.

'I don't know how we're going to get back up,' said Mika breathlessly. She could tell he was scared.

'It'll be fine,' she said. 'Think of it as stretching in the opposite direction.'

That day, in the cave, the whole complicated human world disappeared. There was only the view of the desert, red-hilled, speckled-yellow, shimmering with heat.

'It's kind of like a secret place, like your tunnel in your old house,' she said and the words sounded loud and unnecessary in that place.

'Yeah,' he said, unusually quiet for Mika. He drew a spiral in the red dirt and Pip watched his finger.

She waited for a story but it didn't come; he simply stared out at the desert. They sat side by side not speaking, and the silence felt good.

'I feel like I'm sitting in the hill's mouth,' said Mika at last.

'What?' she said.

Mika laughed softly. 'That's what it feels like.'

Pip giggled.

'Hope it's not hungry,' she said.

That day they found a black shard of stone, shiny and smooth, and it was the first of the stones she'd take home. He'd picked it up after they'd climbed back up from the cave reluctantly, him behind her, following each of her footholds.

'You can almost see your reflection in it,' he said, holding it to his face then handing it to her. 'I think it's a meteor. I bet a million dollars it's a meteor.'

'It's cool,' she said. 'We should show it to someone.'

'Maybe,' he said.

When she went to give it back to him, he put up his hand.

'You keep it,' he said.

'You found it,' said Pip.

They'd found so much that day. Pip felt full with all they'd found: the stone, silence, a whole secret cave.

'I want you to have it,' he said.

SOMETIMES WHEN MATT WOKE ON SUNDAY mornings it was like a bear waking up from hibernation. As though all that loud television and all those beer cans were months ago. He made a snuffling noise first and then a grunting noise. Then he grunted and snuffled together. He got up and, as he got up, he roared. He slammed the toilet door and the house shook. He fumbled around in the bathroom, coughing and spitting. He ran the tap hard so that it screeched in protest.

Sometimes. Mostly. Nearly always.

Pip hoped it wasn't this morning. They sat, Laura and her, knees touching with the sleeping Little Fella between them. The songs were dried up and the tears were gone. Laura was looking at him with fascination. He was curled tight as an ammonite, his head deep inside his tail, which was plump now, deep black, shimmering with the deepest blue.

'We should go,' Pip said. Her ears were tuned to her mother and Matt's bedroom, listening for any sound.

'Where?'

'I know a cave,' said Pip.

'A cave?' Laura said and Pip could almost see her picturing it, dark and foul-smelling, dripping.

'It's a nice cave,' said Pip quickly.

'Okay.'

Pip placed the pink doll's blanket in her backpack and lowered the sleeping Little Fella onto it, then put the backpack on. It felt natural, that action, the weight of him. A dragon on her back, sleeping. She should probably have a role too, the way Laura was a True Dragon Singer, but she didn't know what hers should be. Dragon Carrier? That wasn't right. Dragon Saver? No. Dragon Carer? Weird. Dragon Keeper. Definitely not right, because she knew he couldn't be kept, although that last name made the breath catch in her throat.

'Umm, you can't go in your pyjamas,' giggled Laura.

And suddenly they were just Pip and Laura, two very different girls from Grade Five.

'I knew that,' Pip laughed.

She put the backpack down and slipped out of her pyjama shorts and shirt while Laura turned her back. She put on her old shorts and a green T-shirt and then slipped her feet into her grubby old Dunlop sneakers. She grabbed her hair into a rough ponytail without brushing it.

'Do you want me to braid that?' offered Laura.

Pip made a face.

'Seriously, it's pretty bad,' said Laura.

Pip shrugged. She sat back on the bed and waited.

'Brush?' asked Laura.

'Oh yeah, it's somewhere here,' said Pip. She opened the rock drawer by accident, closed it just as quickly.

Laura eyed the brush she was handed with distaste, but she went to work. She brushed, divided, started to weave.

'Do you have any ribbon?'

'Um, no,' said Pip.

Laura sighed.

Life without ribbons, Pip could almost hear her thinking. *What would that possibly be like?* The skin on her left arm tightened, creaked, released. She hadn't told Laura about that yet.

'There,' said Laura when she was done. 'That's so perfect. Sometimes dirty hair helps with braiding.'

'Oh,' said Pip, examining herself in the wardrobe mirror. Her head was so ridiculously neat it made her grimace.

'Don't you like it?'

'I like it,' said Pip.

She had the backpack on again when they heard Matt roar. It stopped Laura's smile. He roared Pip's mother's name: 'MEL!' It was wet and throaty and it made the walls shake.

'We've got to get out of here,' said Pip.

In the kitchen Laura unzipped her backpack and Pip threw in supplies: more Weet-Bix, arrowroot biscuits, muesli bars. She had almost completely depleted the pantry's supplies. They ran out the front door, past her mum, who was sitting on the stairs in the morning sun, ignoring the roar.

'Hey,' she said as they rushed past and picked up their bikes. 'Nice hair.'

'I did it,' said Laura.

'Were you both singing before? It was beautiful.'

'Yeah, we were writing a song together, weren't we Pip?' lied Laura. Pip was proud of her – this lie sounded much more believable than the last one.

'We'll be back much later,' said Pip.

'Where are you going?'

'Just Laura's house and maybe for a ride.'

Her mother seemed about to ask for more details but there was another roar from inside.

'MEL!'

Pip's mum flinched, stood up, smiled.

'Well, you look like two peas in a pod,' she said and walked inside and Pip and Laura were pedalling, away, as fast as they could into the sunlight.

MRS JARVINEN HAD SAID MIKA AND PIP were two peas in a pod. Cut from the same cloth. Tarred with the same brush. Birds of a feather that flocked together.

'Are you sure you're not related?' she asked them.

That amused Mika no end. 'Imagine,' he said. 'Maybe we are. Maybe way back, like so far back, we share some DNA. My mum did DNA at uni. She knew all about it. Pip, it would explain why I got on with you from the beginning. Have you got a family tree, Nan?'

'No, no time for family trees,' said Mrs Jarvinen.

'You?' he asked Pip.

'I don't think so,' she said. 'My grandma and grandpa live in Townsville and maybe I could ask them one day.'

Across the hills, the desert, the channel country, the Great Dividing Range. They always seemed far, far away.

'Your grandmother is a raving lunatic,' Matt had said to Pip once.

'No, she's not,' Pip had said in return. Her grandmother was kind. She had blue eyes like Pip's mother and she liked to hug and she did Zumba in her living room and she kept all her wildlife-caring supplies on a high shelf in the laundry.

He'd laughed.

'You wouldn't have a clue,' he'd said, like Pip was an ant he wanted to squish and the memory of her grandmother was an ant he wanted to squish too. And anything that didn't belong to him was something to squish; anything that her mum loved other than him, like sea creatures or floaty maxi dresses or speaking to people – all had to be squished.

'Townsville!' cried Mika. 'Didn't you say you had a

sister in Townsville, Nan? We are *so* related. What about your real dad's family?'

'He came from Western Australia,' said Pip.

'That's where my mum went,' said Mika. 'So. Many. Freaky. Similarities.'

Pip wondered where the dotted line on his folded map of Australia had reached. She couldn't tell if he was being silly or serious.

Mrs Jarvinen told him to stop being silly.

Pip stood beside Laura Denning at their hill and even if she had the same hair, she didn't feel like a pea in a pod. But she also wasn't alone and she was glad for that. They left their bikes in the ditch beside the road and climbed through the orange rock and spinifex. It was still quiet even though the sun was up properly now, showing its muscles, burning all the heads of trees and heating up the roads. Up above, hawks were circling slowly in the sky.

Laura is heavy-footed for a dancer, Pip thought. She crashed along the path behind Pip, not noticing the striped skinks that slipped away into cracks. She startled several grass wrens that erupted from their hiding places in the spinifex.

'You don't have to be so loud,' said Pip.

'Mum always says to be loud in the bush so it scares snakes away,' said Laura. 'I didn't know there were caves here. How do you even know that kind of stuff?'

'We used to explore,' said Pip. 'You find things when you explore.'

'You and Mika?' Laura asked.

'Yes.'

'My mum said it was his mum's fault,' said Laura.

Pip let that one slide, kept walking.

'And that he was never supervised properly.'

Pip turned so quickly that Laura bumped into her. She knew that's what all those kinds of people said about Mika but they didn't know anything. They didn't know his mother. They didn't know *him*. To them, he was just a scruffy boy who never went home after school until the sun was deep behind the hills. He was a shadow they saw sometimes on the way home from picking up children from dance class or softball or boy scouts. They didn't know his million stories. They didn't know all his sixth sense feelings. They didn't know he carried the universe in his backpack.

She didn't have any words.

'I'm only repeating what other people say,' Laura said. 'Not me.'

'Well your mum didn't know him.'

Pip turned again and kept climbing.

'You're not the only one who misses him,' said Laura. 'Everyone does. Every single person.'

That made Pip stop again, although she didn't turn.

'Over the top and then down, hidden, on the other side,' she said to change the subject. 'Come on. That's the tricky part.'

She worried about Laura and the backwards climb and drop. Pip and Mika had climbed down so many times that they could have done it with their eyes closed.

They stopped and Laura unzipped the backpack to check on Little Fella.

'He's awake,' she said. 'Hello, Little Fella. I think he's hungry again. Are we nearly there?'

'We're here.'

Laura looked at where the path ended and the sunlit air began.

'What do you mean?'

Pip went first and showed Laura what to do. All the while Little Fella butted his head against the backpack zipper. *Nearly there, Little Fella.*

'Move your foot to the right, a little more. That's your left. Stretch.'

Laura made terrified noises.

Not only did Pip have a dragon to save, she now had a useless girl to worry about. She should have done it alone.

Don't be so hard on her, said Mika very clearly in her ear. *Remember me on that first day?*

'Laura, listen to me. Once you move your foot to the right and stretch it gets really easy, I promise you,' she said. 'I wouldn't lie. I've done it so many times.'

Laura stretched her leg and found the foothold.

'See, from there it's easy,' said Pip. 'And I promise it is much better going back up.'

'I don't like it,' said Laura and it sounded like she was crying.

'That's it; you've already done the next step, you're nearly there. When you get to the next foot place you can jump. Just don't jump out too far or you'll fall off the whole hill.'

'I hate you,' said Laura.

'Down. Jump now. See how close you are?'

'That's not close!'

'It's a metre and a half, max! Jump!'

'I think I've broken my ankle,' said Laura when she landed.

'Don't be a wimp.'

In the cool mouth of the cave, Pip unzipped the backpack. Little Fella's head was straight out and he was full of beans. It made them laugh and forget about their previous words. He crawled into Pip's arms, nuzzled and rattled and then scooted the small distance to Laura and did the same to her.

'Oh,' said Laura, and Pip reckoned she had a song ready to come up. 'I just don't get it,' said Laura, holding her chest like she might be able to stop it happening.

There was no stopping it though. She was already singing by the time she got to the word *it*. Little Fella rolled onto his back in her lap as she sang. Pip searched inside herself for the jealousy and couldn't find it. Her skin stiffened momentarily, though. It wasn't only her left arm, it was her left leg too, her thigh and her kneecap. Her hand suddenly weighed as much as a small car. She checked again for signs of scales and then remembered Mika's words.

Some things you can't think.

She breathed out. Her skin creaked, released. The heaviness in her hand lessened.

Laura, the Dragon Singer, watched Pip examining her arm briefly then returned to singing to Little Fella's wings. He seemed to go limp with Laura's songs. She could do anything with him. Laura rolled him over and spread out his wings and sang along the veins. She removed pieces of sticky tape here and there. She undid two paddle-pop sticks. She cried some tears although she was smiling as she cried. Laura looked really beautiful like that; mending dragon wings, crying and smiling.

Pip watched her, mushed the Weet–Bix, let her own tears drip.

Neither of them heard the footfall above. Not for one second did they hear the footsteps, or the breathing, or the soft giggle.

When Archie Morgan jumped down into the cave it was theatrical. He must have wanted to make a grand entrance, a great big fat 'TA DA!' just so that Laura and Pip would be completely impressed by his supreme stealth and ninja abilities. He dropped down from the overhang and into their view, his arms outstretched.

Then he screamed.

THEY MIGHT HAVE HEARD HIM IN CLONCURRY.
He screamed so loud and with such an expression of horror on his face that it made Laura scream too. She screamed mid-song, hands up to her face. Archie leaped backwards and began to fall. That was another scream, right there, from everyone, even Pip. Even Little Fella who leaped into the air, let out a small screech-hiss, all while Pip lurched forwards and grabbed Archie before he fell, dragging him onto the ground, spraying dirt and pebbles.

Little Fella landed right in front of him, so Archie screamed again. A wobbly, half-hearted scream. Laura again too, for good measure. Pip opened her arms for the dragon, and he raced into them.

'What?' said Archie. One word. He had no breath for more.

Pip grabbed the pink doll's blanket from the backpack and covered Little Fella. She could feel his little heart racing and his small chest heaving.

'You can't creep up on people like that!' she shouted, deliberately not answering his question. 'Seriously.'

'Seriously,' said Laura. 'It's against the law.'

'There's no law,' whispered Archie, his eyes on the doll's blanket. 'What *is* that?'

He asked it like he really didn't want to know, a whiny twang to his voice.

'What's what?' asked Pip, keeping her face blank.

'That thing!' cried Archie. 'I mean . . . what?'

'There's no thing,' said Laura.

Archie got to his feet. Pip couldn't tell what he was going to do. She stared at his old sneakers, holes in both toes.

'There is a thing under that blanket,' he said softly, trying to contain his fear. Pip knew it was leaking out of him everywhere. 'I saw the thing. It's under that blanket.'

Laura made a sighing noise.

'Archie,' she said quietly. 'You really shouldn't have followed us.'

'How'd you even know we were here?' Pip said. 'How'd you even know about this cave?'

'I saw you on the crossing and I followed you. You're pretty easy to follow,' he whispered, eyes not moving from the blanket and the lump beneath it.

'But how'd you know about this cave?' spat Pip. It was Mika's and her cave. She scrunched up her face with anger and her eyes burned with hot tears. No one knew about it.

Archie shrugged at that.

'Chill, dude,' he said.

'He can't unsee it, Pip,' said Laura.

Why was she even here with them? This was her dragon. *Her* dragon that *she* was meant to save. And why was Laura now the Dragon Singer and wise one? *He can't unsee it, Pip.*

'Yes, he can,' said Pip. 'He really can. I'll push him off the edge.'

Archie was watching the blanket. His eyes flicked up to Pip.

'You wouldn't,' said Archie. 'You stopped me falling. And I'm much stronger than you, Pipsqueak.'

There was a slight tremor of uncertainty to his words, though. He took a big breath, puffed out his chest to cover the tremor.

'Look,' he said. 'I didn't mean to creep up on you. I mean, I did. But I knew you were up to something. Why are you even crying? I mean, Laura, Pip. You're not even friends.'

'Yes, we are,' said Laura, forcefully.

'We are,' said Pip, wiping at the hot tears. She did want to push him off the edge.

Archie laughed and shook his head.

'Okay, then,' he said. 'You're friends. I'm not going to tell anyone. No one at all. That thing. I know it's not a bat. Is it a bat? What's the big deal about hiding a bat? But if it *is* a bat, you shouldn't be playing with it because they can kill you with a disease. My Aunty Chez told me. She got bitten once and had to have ten injections.'

'It's a bat, Archie,' said Laura.

'Dudes!' said Archie, kicking the ground. 'I *know* it's not a bat.'

'Well why are you giving us safety tips for looking after bats?' cried Pip. She knew she couldn't keep Little Fella under the blanket for long. He was restlessly nudging against her chest.

'I won't tell,' he said.

Laura and Pip kept sitting there. Archie kept standing. A stand-off that might go on forever.

'Archie,' Pip said softly, her voice hoarse with tears, 'you really shouldn't have followed us.'

Archie took his place between them, his back to the day outside the cave.

'I promise,' he said.

'Don't make promises you can't keep,' said Laura. 'It's just that you'll ruin everything if you tell anyone else. All we are trying to do is save it. Make it well. We can't keep it. It isn't ours.'

Pip slowly uncovered Little Fella cradled against her chest. His lava lamp eyes immediately found Archie but he only made the maraca noise, nuzzled under Pip's neck and rolled over for more belly scratching.

'Where'd you get him?' said Archie quietly.

'I didn't get him,' said Pip. 'I found him. Down the creek. He was nearly dead.'

'When?'

'Four nights ago. I saved him with arrowroot biscuits.'

Four nights only? It seemed like a lifetime had passed. The days had yawned into years. Arrowroot biscuits seemed a thing of the far ago past. Even Laura arriving in her room. Her startled scream. Her singing together of the wings.

'Where'd he come from?' said Archie. His words were breathless.

'I don't think he's from here,' said Pip.

She placed Little Fella on the ground. He swayed on his little legs, his belly round from Weet-Bix. He trotted unsteadily to Laura and climbed into her lap. He spread his wings and waited.

'Oh,' said Laura. Her deep, sad *oh*, and the song came up.

It was beautiful, even more beautiful than the last one, if that could be possible. It made Pip wipe at her eyes straightaway. She saw the hairs on Archie's arms rise.

'What's going on?' he whispered. 'That's freaking me out.'

'She's a Dragon Singer,' said Pip, crumpling her nose apologetically. 'Turns out.'

'Oh,' said Archie.

Pip watched him to see if he would cry, but all she noticed was the wave upon wave of goosebumps on his brown arms.

'Fudge-nuggets,' he said quietly under his breath.

THE SECOND STONE THAT MIKA GAVE HER was a little piece of pink quartz with seams of fool's gold.

'You've got to keep this one,' she said.

'Nah, it's got your name written all over it,' he said.

'How?'

'Pink and gold,' he said. 'All girly.'

Her cheeks ignited and she punched him on the arm, which made him laugh even more.

'Jokes,' he howled with laughter as she kicked him in the shin. 'Only jokes.'

Pip washed it at the waterhole. No matter where they went, they always returned to the waterhole, that tiny deep pool that held the many reflections of the sky: the fierce sun at noon, the electric blue morning sky, the late afternoon's golds. The pool held shadows. It held stars. It held the moon, Pip was sure of it, although she had never seen it. She would have to be there at exactly the right time at night, on exactly the right night, when the earth was tilted just the right way.

They had *adventures*. Mika's word. They'd found the cave. They walked all the way along the dry river to the Junction in search of the deadly whirlpool but found only more dry river. They spied on some boys who rode BMX bikes on the bulldust road, following them soundlessly and crouched in the yellow grassed overhang of the riverbank. Wherever they went they kept an eye open for bunyip clues: drag marks, footprints, bunyip poo. She took him to the haunted place, a place of tall, straight gum trees where the air was different, where it was so quiet that your ears hummed, and when they got spooked by a branch snapping, they ran, first shrieking, then laughing so hard that Pip couldn't breathe. But after each adventure they always returned to the waterhole.

'I wonder how deep it is,' Mika always said.

'It's just deep,' said Pip. That should be enough.

She watched the flock of corellas on the opposite bank, making a ruckus beneath the silver box trees.

'What about one of those laser measuring tapes that carpenters use, maybe we could shine it down into the water?'

Pip didn't know any carpenters and she was pretty sure Mika didn't either.

'It's just deep,' she said again, softly.

'I bet if you had scuba diving equipment you could get to the bottom,' said Mika.

That day with the pink stone held in her palm, catching the late afternoon light, it became their telling place. The cover story of bunyip searching slipped. Teeth, claws, shaggy fur, scales, blackness, greyness, brownness, drippingness, all disintegrated. Pip taunted him by placing her feet into the water at dusk and smiling sweetly at him. He clapped his hands on his head and moaned.

'Seriously, Pip.'

Bunyip stories changed into other supernatural

stories of which Mika possessed a wealth. He told her about a place where smudgy faces appeared in a tiled floor, their mouths open, as though they were silently screaming. He told her about the true story of a poltergeist in Germany. He told her about a range of headless haunted things and headless haunted things seemed what he was expert at. Headless ladies, headless monks, headless headmasters, headless brides, headless grooms.

And the headless things dripped away to bad men. And then a short story, an excerpt of what he was hiding from in the secret tunnel in his house in Oxley. Cops once. The Department of Children's Services on the day his mother put him on the train. But mostly a guy called Marty who was really bad.

'He was, like . . . think of the scariest man you can think of, Pip.' Pip thought of Matt. 'Now multiply it by one hundred.'

Matt didn't need to be multiplied.

She didn't say that. She waited, holding her breath, for Mika's scary man.

'So, like, really muscly, lots of tats. Two full sleeves. He always took his shirt off. He had his hair shaved except for this bit here.'

Mika pointed to the front of his head.

'Bad teeth,' he added.

Pip couldn't quite form an image of him, despite all that, and she tried hard. She closed her eyes.

'Say it again,' she said.

Mika repeated his description.

'He had a really deep voice. Like, when you heard it, it made your heart stop.'

Pip knew about that.

'He'd come in and he was always going fast. He walked fast like he could just bash right through a wall and his fists were always like this and his mouth was always like this.'

Pip had to open her eyes to see what he was doing.

'And he was my mum's boyfriend,' he said. Hesitated. 'Then she had to get away from him.'

'He sounds terrible,' Pip said, because she could only hear about him, not see him at all. All she could see was Matt.

Then that story closed up and Mika started talking about other things again. Jokes at first. Mika could be a walking joke book if the time was right. *What do you get if you cross a snowman and a shark?* Frostbite. *What do you get if you cross a cat with a tree?* A cat-a-logue. Even though she laughed she wanted to say: tell me the story of why you were put on the train.

He changed the subject to Sagittarius A then, the black hole located at the centre of the Milky Way. The place he told Laura he'd come from.

'We're probably all going to get sucked into it one day,' he said, cheerfully. 'I mean, not us, the world, our sun. We won't be here anymore. We'll be long gone.'

Pip moaned. He put bunyips in waterholes and star-gobbling black holes at the centre of the Milky Way.

'Yeah,' he said after a while when she didn't take the bait, 'Sagittarius A is going to hoover us all up.'

She hit him on the arm, hard.

'Ouch,' he said, laughing.

Then: 'This place is special. Can you feel it?'

The sun was slipping down behind the trees and the corellas rose swiftly from the earth in unison; in one great rushing uplift they looped in a circle above Pip and Mika's heads, hundreds upon hundreds of birds, the air filled with their joyous chattering and screeching.

'Yeah,' said Pip, smiling, when the birds had disappeared into the evening sky and it was quiet again.

At home, Matt made her show him what was in her hand. She'd opened her palm to reveal the pink and gold stone.

'Shouldn't bring crap like that home,' he said. 'It's filthy.'

It was only because it was something that belonged to her, not him. He couldn't stand that. He went to snatch it from her.

'Don't!' she said, and her voice was loud and it sounded the way her mother called out that word late at night. 'Mika gave it to me.'

'Your boyfriend,' he sneered. 'Bit young for a boyfriend, aren't you?'

'Leave her alone, Matt,' said her mum. 'He's her good friend.'

'Good friend,' laughed Matt, like he'd never heard of such a thing.

ARCHIE LAY DOWN ON HIS BELLY, MESMERISED,
his head propped up on his hands, watching
Little Fella sleeping. The song had been sung and his
wings mended some more and they were all quiet.
Archie hadn't cried. He hadn't spoken either. He
hadn't tried to speak over it or about it, he had just
sat very still during the singing, his eyes downcast.
It wasn't what Pip had expected. She'd expected
boy stuff. Dragon expert boy stuff. When Laura had
finished her song, even she'd looked at him, raising
her eyebrows. A what-have-you-got-to-say-about-
that expression on her face. He might've wanted to
ask a million different questions – *how'd you know he*

liked that? Where'd you learn that tune? Except Archie didn't ask any.

It gave Pip hope.

It worried her, too.

'Haven't you got anything to say?' she asked into the silence as he lay there gazing at Little Fella. Laura had curled herself into a ball in the shade, exhausted.

'Yeah, well,' he said. Pip could tell he wanted to touch the dragon. Every sinew in his body wanted to touch it. She seemed to have a feeling for these things now. Archie kept his hands exactly where they were.

'Yeah, well?' repeated Pip.

'Course I have,' he said. 'But . . .'

'But what?'

'But I'm just thinking,' he said. 'I mean. About stuff. About why he might be here. Where he came from. That kind of stuff.'

'He's lost,' said Laura from her curled ball.

'Obviously,' said Archie and there was no malice in it.

'Lost,' said Pip quietly, and her skin tightened again. Arm, leg, chest. It was painful now, that tightness. A clenching. She sighed when it released.

'How do we help him?' asked Archie. His first real question. 'I mean you're singing to him and doing stuff to his wings and you're . . .'

He turned to Pip. It still had no name, her dragon-saving. She was with the dragon. That was how she'd say it. He was in her and she was in him. Somehow. The way she'd briefly heard things differently, then smelled them differently, and now the way her skin was tighter everywhere, and her hand a dense mass and a feeling inside her that she couldn't explain.

Even though there wasn't a mark left on her hand, something in them had mixed.

'Yeah, I don't know what my job is called,' said Pip.

The sun made its way up past the cave ceiling, cast them all in shade.

What would Archie's purpose be?

Pip knew he wanted to touch Little Fella and he was stopping himself so maybe that was it.

Not a poke type of touch, a tender touch. The small cave was thrumming with that energy.

'You can touch him,' said Pip.

They rode towards Laura's house and stopped at the bottom of her street. Laura explained the plan. In quick, steal food from the pantry, out again. Pip smiled to hear Laura speak like that. She liked the new dragon singing, stealing, lying Laura.

'Let me check on him,' said Archie. Pip could tell he had the bug bad. He wanted to keep gazing at Little Fella, the way he had in the cave, the way he'd tentatively offered his forearm to the dragon and Little Fella had cautiously climbed on. He needed to do that, and keep doing that, the way Laura had returned that morning with dark rings beneath her eyes, needing to sing.

Laura peered into the backpack too.

'Sleeping,' she said.

When they were at her front gate she said, 'If we get caught just act normal.'

That made Pip smile again. There was nothing normal about Archie and Pip walking up Laura Denning's garden path.

And Laura's house was something else. It was a mine company house like Pip's, the exact same style; same patio, same floor plan, but everything else was different. Laura's house was prim. It held its patio in a haughty way. There were bowls of petunias on the front steps. The screen door didn't slam; it had some kind of mechanism that made it close slowly, politely. Inside the air conditioning was so cool that Pip shivered and Archie gasped.

Everything was in the right place: fluffy cushions, golden Buddhas, a little fountain trickling on a small table. There were wood-carved words here and there: 'HOME'. 'LOVE'. 'SERENITY'. It made Pip feel weird.

'I feel weird,' she whispered.

'Shhhh,' said Laura.

Archie was tiptoeing in a comical way that made Pip giggle.

'Is that you, Laura?' A voice came from the kitchen, and Laura's mum walked out.

'Oh,' she said.

It was a surprised *oh*. She recovered herself quickly, Pip had to admit. And really, she had a right to an even bigger *Oh*. They were all covered in dirt from sitting in a cave, and Laura had lots of spinifex scratches on her legs. Also, there was some dragon poo on her white skirt.

'Hi,' said Archie, smiling his huge smile.

Pip waved a small, unsure wave.

'We've been climbing in the hills,' said Laura.

'Oh darling, darling,' said her mum, 'you shouldn't go places like that without telling me. Which hills? I thought you went to Tiffany's house.'

'The hill behind the roller-dome,' said Pip, helpfully. 'It's a fairly normal hill.'

Mrs Denning smiled kindly in return although Pip didn't think it was particularly convincing. Mrs Denning had blonde hair with salon waves. She looked like a news presenter. She smelled of some delicious perfume that tickled Pip's nose.

'Do you want some cookies?' she asked.

'Sure,' said Pip, shifting her focus to feel the weight of the dragon in her backpack. This was, she decided, the worst idea anyone had ever had in the entire history of the universe.

'Yes please,' said Archie.

'Mum makes the best cookies,' said Laura. 'Come on, I'll show you where the bathroom is.'

'I live in exactly the same house,' said Pip.

'So do I,' said Archie.

'Oh yeah,' said Laura and she giggled. 'I forgot.'

'Maybe leave those backpacks outside, they're pretty dirty,' called Mrs Denning after them.

That stopped them in their tracks.

'No, they've got important stuff inside,' said Laura, turning. 'Promise we won't put them on the bed.'

Mrs Denning didn't appear pleased with that. She didn't appear pleased with any of it. Not the backpack, not the hill-climbing, not the dirty faces, not the new friends – especially the new friends. Still, she fixed her newsreader-cookie-baking smile back on.

'Okay,' she said. 'Not on the bed. You have a lilac bedspread, remember?'

In the bathroom:

'We shouldn't have come,' said Pip.

Archie was wide-eyed, taking in all the white fluffy towels and matching bathrobes and perched wooden words that read 'RELAX', 'UNWIND', 'CALM'. He pointed to Pip and then to the wooden word 'RELAX' and then cracked up silently at his joke. Pip narrowed her eyes at him. Archie unzipped the backpack and peered at Little Fella's sleeping form.

'It'll be fine,' said Laura. 'Charlee will wake up soon. When Mum's gone from the kitchen, we'll grab the stuff.'

'What if Little Fella wakes up first?'

'He won't,' said Laura, Dragon Singer and expert on dragon sleep patterns.

'We have to be quick,' said Pip.

'Cookies won't take long.'

'I think you'll find they're called biscuits. "Cookies" is American,' said Archie.

Laura rolled her eyes.

Pip glimpsed Laura's room as they went back down the hallway. Laura's bedspread was purple with pink flowers, pink and purple cushions arranged perfectly, her pink pyjamas laid out like she was a princess.

They took their places at the dining room table, the backpack between Pip's legs under the table. Mrs Denning served them like at a cafe, with china plates and serviettes. She gave them ice with their juice from the icemaker on their shiny silver fridge.

'There you go,' she said. She sat with them but didn't have juice or biscuits. 'Your mum's Melanie, right?'

'Melissa,' said Pip.

'Melissa, sorry. And your dad is . . .'

'He's not my dad,' said Pip. 'Matt.'

Mrs Denning kept smiling right the way through that.

'I think Matt works in a different area to your dad, Laura, but they have the same sort of job,' said Mrs Denning.

'Cool,' said Laura.

'Nice biscuit,' said Pip.

'Glad you like it,' said Mrs Denning.

She turned to Archie. 'And your mum is Stacey, right? From the tuckshop.'

'Yeah, she's the tuckshop convenor,' said Archie, his

mouth full of biscuit. 'I really want her to let there be red frogs again. I'm fighting for it.'

It looked like there was more to that story but his mouth was too full. Mrs Denning interrupted anyway.

'So, just so you know Pip – is that what I call you? Pip or Pippa?'

'Pip,' said Pip.

'And Archie, just so you know,' Mrs Denning continued, carefully, 'Laura isn't allowed to run wild. She has to ask where she can go *before* she goes and she definitely can't just go climbing hills. There's snakes and god knows what else up those hills. We all know what happened . . .'

'It's not their fault,' said Laura, quickly.

'I know. I'm letting *them* know *our* rules. In case you all have a play date again.'

The words 'play date' hung between them at the table like a tacky helium balloon. Pip had an image of them in the cave, Laura singing to the dragon's wings and tears dripping down her own face. The way the mouth of the cave held them and the way, even after

Archie had arrived, they had re-sorted themselves. How he had touched that dragon with quiet tenderness, running his fingers over its snout, its tiny nubs of horns, its claws.

Play date.

She heard Mika's laugh, far, far, away.

The biscuit is okay, Pip thought, *but it isn't the best.* Her mum made better biscuits, actually. She stared at the pretty plate. She knew what was coming next.

'Next time, maybe Pip's mum or Archie's mum can call and arrange a time and place,' said Mrs Denning. 'You told me you were going to Tiffany's this morning, honey.'

Laura shrugged, stared at her plate, her face turning red.

Little Fella rattled. A really loud rattle. Pip's heart stopped.

Archie coughed loudly. He tried to add a rattle to it. It sounded more gurgly. Mrs Denning stared at him in shock.

He did it again when Little Fella started rattling again.

Maybe Mrs Denning was going to say something else but right then the baby woke and she smiled her cool, slightly confused smile again before standing up.

'Quick,' said Laura when she was gone. They rushed into the kitchen and piled tins into the mauve backpack. Pumpkin baby food. Alphagetti. Custard. A box of Weet-Bix, unopened.

Biscuits – arrowroot and lemon custard.

'You wait outside,' instructed Laura.

Pip and Archie rushed out onto the patio, the screen door closing politely behind them.

'Hi Charlee,' they heard Laura say. 'Mum, I'm going to ride Pip and Archie back to their houses, and then I'm going to drop Tiffany's dance shoes to her like I was supposed to this morning. She was at the gymnastics competition again. Can I play with her for a while?'

'Yes, you can. Good girl,' said Mrs Denning.

Tiffany. Correct non-hill-climbing-never-running-wild friend.

THEY SAT ON THE CONCRETE CIRCLE WHERE the old water tower once stood. All that was left there was the detritus of rusted pipes and broken glass and around its perimeter a ring of long yellow grass. The place Mika had said was a landing pad for alien spacecraft.

I'm glad you're still here, she said silently to him.

She could feel him. Not close but still there. She was worried what he might think of her new dragon-saving friends.

Archie mushed the Weet-Bix and then had a turn at feeding Little Fella, who had woken extra-frisky. He'd exploded upwards out of the backpack with gleaming mischievous eyes. Pip put him on the ground and he ran in a little circle, his legs much sturdier, leaving claw marks in the dust. He head-butted Laura right in the tummy where she was sitting cross-legged and they all laughed at his antics.

'He's the best thing I've ever seen in my entire life,' said Archie.

If Mrs Denning's words had stung him, he didn't show it. Pip was still stung. Mrs Denning needed a wooden word sign that said *I have a stick up my bum.* She would have said that to Archie if Laura wasn't there.

Laura was smiling at Little Fella, touching his wings. She wasn't singing though.

'They look good,' Laura said, 'all the little tears are nearly gone. I'm going to leave the last few paddle-pop sticks.'

'No song?' asked Pip.

'I can feel it, but it doesn't want to come out,' she said, choosing her words carefully, trying to understand it. 'And . . .'

'And?'

'It's way down deep. Like, I can only just feel it.'

'Maybe it means it's fading,' said Archie. 'Like you don't need to sing it anymore.'

'The healing song?' asked Pip.

'Yeah, like maybe the healing is done,' said Archie.

Pip waited for Laura to argue, to grow petulant, because that's what she'd be like at school. If someone took something away from her – her crown, her position at the head of the line, her job of going to get the tuckshop bucket.

Laura didn't say anything for a while, then: 'Maybe.'

The sun was nearly touching the hills and Tiffany's ballet shoes were still in Laura's backpack and Pip knew she'd be in big trouble. Like she'd probably never been in trouble before.

'Yeah, maybe,' Laura said again. Almost a whisper.

After he'd eaten his Weet-Bix, they watched Little Fella watching the galahs that came sweeping in great flocks and then the wild budgerigars darting at high speed. He sat on his hind legs with his little black snout lifted to the air. His scales were dark but as the sun slipped further down and bathed their circle in gold, the deeper blue hue of the scales shimmered.

'I think he can fly,' said Archie quietly.

'I don't think he can,' said Pip quickly, because she was remembering the incident with the hawk.

They sat in silence for a while.

'Pip,' said Archie, 'I think he can. I kind of . . .'

Pip shook her head, sighed.

'You kind of what?' asked Laura.

'Dunno,' said Archie and he picked some gravel up, pretending to be interested in it. 'Yeah, I just reckon I know how to get him to fly. And I reckon he needs to know how to fly.'

Pip checked the sky, which was growing dark at the edges.

'Show us then,' she said.

'Be careful,' said Laura.

'I will, I will,' said Archie quietly. He got up, looked at the sky himself, then squatted.

He offered his forearm to Little Fella who was sniffing the coming night, and without any hesitation, he climbed on.

'I mean really careful,' said Pip, searching the sky for the one hundredth time. There were no eagles or hawks, only the odd pink galah late home, skimming across the deepening blue.

'Shhhh now,' said Archie. 'Watch.'

He had Little Fella on his forearm and he extended his other arm out straight. 'Jump,' he said. No singing. No strange dragon language.

'Come on,' he said, quietly. Little Fella watched Archie's eyes. Archie pointed his eyes to his out-stretched arm. The dragon didn't really have to jump because the space was quite close. It was more of a stretch than anything, but he spanned the space in one quick movement, a half-hop.

The skin on Pip's left arm momentarily tightened and released.

'Nice work, little dude,' said Archie when Little Fella had done it and then he moved his extended arm further away. Again, he said, 'Jump.'

This time Little Fella did have to leap and with the small jump his wings opened, and two paddle-pop sticks rained free. He made the distance comfortably.

'Dude, you are awesome,' said Archie.

'Good work, Little Fella,' said Laura.

Pip was staring at her arm. She'd seen something. She'd seen a sudden shimmering. A nanosecond luminescence that was attached to the ache.

Or was she imagining that? She must have been imagining it.

She stared at the sky, the concrete, remembered Little Fella dropped and splatted from that bird's talons. Her hand ached suddenly again and the skin across her chest and thighs tightened, but there was nothing, absolutely nothing shining.

'Careful,' she whispered.

Archie was only concentrating on Little Fella though. He might have been speaking but that was just a cover for what was going on between their eyes. His arm went out further, almost out of Little Fella's sight.

'Jump,' said Archie and he showed Little Fella with his eyes.

Little Fella leaped and this time his wings extended and flapped twice. The remaining paddle-pop stick broke free. The wings were black and delicate as lace, and something in them, diamond-like, shone in the late afternoon sun.

He landed on Archie's arm, looking very pleased with himself.

Pip realised she was holding her breath, and breathed out again.

Laura whispered, 'He's doing it, Pip. He's doing it!'

Now Archie took him on his forearm and dropped the other arm.

'Jump and fly,' he said, only he ran the words together.

Jumpandfly.

Their eyes were locked together, the gold reflected in Archie's brown. Archie threw his glance out in an arc and back to his forearm.

'Jumpandfly,' he said quietly.

Little Fella didn't even hesitate. He leaped from Archie's forearm and his wings flicked open. He flapped them once, twice, three times, then he tilted his body and gracefully curved back towards Archie, wings trembling until he was safely on the forearm.

He wrapped his tail around Archie's wrist, as though to say, *That was scary*.

Laura was clapping, jumping up and down in the dust, and before she even knew it, Pip found herself clapping too. Archie, smiling widely, nodded his head at Little Fella, who seemed ready for another attempt.

Laura grabbed Pip's hand as the dragon readied himself. They were both glad he could fly but also sad, an unfathomable sadness, because at the very same time, as the last of the sun slipped down behind the hills and the thousand glittering lights of the mine winked on, they knew that they were rushing towards the ending of things.

Little Fella stared into Archie's eyes, the Dragon Trainer, and waited.

'Jumpandfly,' said Archie.

ACT III

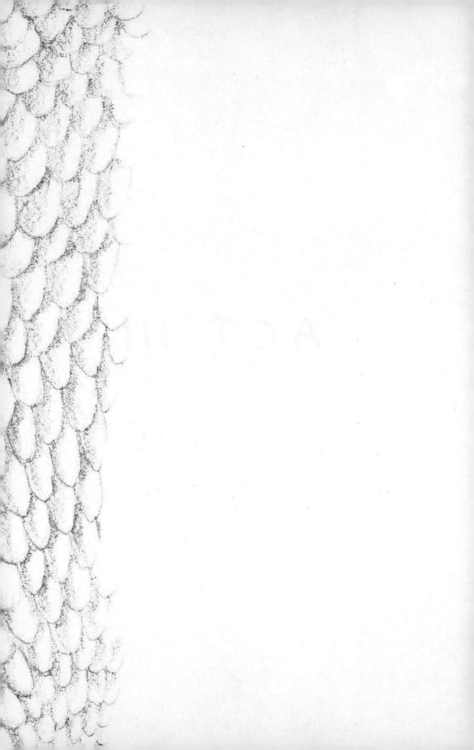

THEY SAID GOODBYE ON THE CORNER OF
her street, Little Fella asleep in Pip's backpack,
exhausted from his first flying lesson. The sun was
gone and Mrs Denning would probably be sending
out a search party.

'I've got to go so bad,' said Laura. She had one peek
at him again. Archie too.

'Is he still sleeping?' asked Pip.

'He's cactus,' said Archie, zipping up the backpack,
carefully.

'Better go,' said Pip.

They were reluctant. All of them.

'What time will we meet tomorrow?'

'Early,' said Laura. 'Oh no, I've got holiday ballet boot camp.'

'Don't go to ballet boot camp,' suggested Pip.

She never in all her life could have thought such a thing would occur. That she would miss Laura. That the next day couldn't be done without her.

'It's only until eleven.'

'Come straight after,' said Archie.

'Where?'

'Our cave,' said Pip.

Our cave.

'Mika,' she whispered as she rode home through the streets. There was only silence.

In Pip's house it was quiet too. There was just one light on in the bedroom.

'Big day?' said her mum from the bedroom.

'I was with Laura all day,' said Pip because she couldn't tell from her mother's voice if she was kind or cranky or sad. She lifted sleeping Little Fella and placed him in the hoodie nest in the wardrobe, hesitated. She took Laura's pink doll's blanket and rested it beside him. She shut the door quietly.

She wondered what it felt like for him. If Little Fella missed his mother. If in that darkness he forgot he was being raised by a girl and her friends, woke searching for something larger, something vaster. Her skin tightened, and she doubled over with the pain of it. She stayed there for several seconds, hands on knees, until it receded. Even though there was no sign of the shimmering in her arm, her heart rate increased at the memory of it so that she had to sit on the bed until it slowed down.

'Hey,' she said at her mother's door.

'Hey,' said her mother, not looking up from the phone.

Women's helpline fare calculator Greyhound Mount Isa to Townsville distance to Hughenden yellow pages car key cutting can I transplant roses in summer apply for a bank loan how to open a $0 fee account in five minutes.

'Where's Matt?' Pip asked.

'He went to the pub.'

'He's got the car?'

'Guess he doesn't trust me with it,' said her mum quietly. She lowered the phone and closed her eyes.

'Does he . . . do you think he knows . . . that we're maybe going to . . .'

'I don't know,' said her mum. 'Probably.'

Pip's heart hurt. It was dragon-saving weary. Her hand was heavy. It contained an *opening*. But . . .

'Mum,' she said. 'We just have to go.'

'I know,' said her mother, putting her hands up to her face and beginning to cry. 'I'm sorry.'

She said 'I'm sorry' again and again until Pip took her hands from her face and held them.

'We have to go fast,' said Pip, whispering even though there was no one there with them. Weary but stronger than she'd ever been. 'When he leaves the car one day.'

'That'll just make things worse, if we take the car,' said her mum, trying to calm her breathing.

'But you paid for heaps of it, all your work money, and he doesn't even let you touch it,' said Pip, growing more forceful. 'He's the one who steals.'

All their happiness. All their laughter. All their air.

Ping went her mother's phone and they both jumped.

'Speak of the devil. He wants us to get a taxi and pick him up,' her mother said and her hands shook. 'And drive him and his bloody car home.'

Pip tried to slow her heart. The *ping* always made her heart go off course, jump and skitter like a runaway train.

She saw he'd sent her mother a selfie, when she put the phone down. He was always sending her selfies, like she might forget who he was. In his selfies he looked like a movie star because he was very good at taking them. Her mother had a whole album of them. He took selfies at work, beside the giant equipment, beside oversized trucks, the sun beating down, and in the reflection of his glasses Pip could see his hand and the phone.

He sent photos when he was reeling Pip's mum back in. When the big freezes were over. When he knew she might be hesitating.

Pip stared at the selfie. He was in the pub and he must have snapped it quick when no one was paying attention. He had a half-smile on his face. His eyes were very blue. In photos Pip's allowed to look at them but in real life he won't let her. He'll look away. As though she was trying to take something from him just by seeing his eyes.

'Come on,' said her mum. 'Let's go.'

THE THIRD STONE MIKA GAVE HER WAS
white quartz. There was a lot of white quartz
lying around but this one was special because it was, if
they used their imagination, egg-shaped, and Mika was
almost certain it was a fossilised dragon's egg. Pip knew
what Matt would say if she said something like that. If
he saw the stone. If he knew who gave it to her. *Is he
your boyfriend?* No. *Why's he always giving you things?* It's
a cool rock. *Do you like boys who are pansies?*

It was the second year of Mika and the second year
of Matt.

The second year of Mika had been good. It was the
sun and bike tyres humming on hot bitumen, it was

exploration and theories on the universe, it was rocks and rock climbing and sitting in caves, it was Ursa growing sleek and sure and Pip relinquishing her twenty-three per cent. It was searching for bunyips, giving up on bunyips, throwing rocks at rusted gallon drums, it was their sunburned legs, soothed by the cool water of the waterhole at dusk. It was lying on their backs at the top of Gallipoli Park, waiting. Waiting for the stars to wink on. Waiting to see UFOs. Waiting for morning so they could see each other again.

The second year of Matt was the opposite.

He'd completely taken over. He'd arrived with his beloved brand-new black four-wheel drive and his stinky deodorants and shaving creams and aftershaves and taken over the bathroom sink first and then he'd taken over the living room, bringing in his big ugly black recliner lounge suite and his giant television. He'd taken over the fridge with all of his beers and his giant slabs of red meat defrosting. It was like a boulder had smashed through the roof and landed in the middle of their house. Pip had to manoeuvre around it, squeeze herself past. Pip had to *adjust*. That's what her mum said. *It will just take a little while to adjust.*

But he didn't just change the physical stuff in their house. He put down roots and changed other things. He changed what Pip's mother wore. He changed what they ate. He changed what they watched on his giant television. He changed how her mother said goodnight to her. She was always rushed. She never sat on the edge of the bed anymore. She never said, 'Sleep tight, Little Swan.'

Quick, quick, turn the light off. Disappear.

He changed everything.

Pip's mum stopped singing and being silly.

Pip's mum stopped dancing.

Pip's mum stopped laughing.

Or she didn't *stop* laughing; she got a new laugh, which Pip had never heard before.

Mika loved Pip's mum's laugh because it reminded him of his own mum.

'It's not her real laugh,' said Pip. 'She had a different laugh before Matt came. Matt ruined everything.'

'He's not that bad, is he?' asked Mika who mostly saw the best in people. He was impressed by Matt's shiny four-wheel drive and the size of his television. And compared to Mika's scary man, Matt probably didn't look that bad.

'Yeah he is,' said Pip. 'On the inside.'

He had the white quartz dragon's egg on the palm of his hand at the waterhole, watching how the sun caught its edges.

'You could keep it and give it to your mum when she comes and gets you,' she said, handing it back to him.

Mika's mum never wrote him a letter. Or phoned. She was driving somewhere in the white station wagon, number plate 966MOP. Or maybe she changed the number plates. Because she had to. Then no one could trace her. Mika made it sound like some kind of spy thriller mystery when he spoke of her. *Mission Impossible*. But he rarely spoke of her. When he did it was bright flashes. She loved strawberry milk. She could draw eyes really well. How she taught Mika to tell the direction of the wind by wetting his finger.

How to tell east from west and north from south.
The names of the stars in the sky: the Southern Cross,
Pleiades, Circinus.

She loved white bread and cheese sandwiches with
the crusts cut off.

She slept with her hands beneath her face in a prayer.

She dyed her hair bright red and she had a nose ring.

She went to university for two years of a science
degree.

Before stuff started happening.

Before Marty.

'She didn't abandon me,' Mika said, suddenly. And
Pip was shocked to see he was crying. There was no
noise, only big tears streaming down his face. He wiped
at them with the back of his arm.

'I didn't think she did,' said Pip.

'I thought you might have,' he laughed, his voice
changed by the tears, still crying. 'She just wanted me
to be safe.'

'No. I never did,' said Pip, grabbing his hands with
her own, the dragon egg stone deep inside. 'I promise.
I didn't.'

He shook his head. Unable to speak. She kept holding until he was breathing again and the tears were gone. All that time she'd thought he'd chosen her but he'd been waiting for her to choose him.

He handed her back the dragon's egg.

'Maybe it will hatch in your rock drawer?' he said, washing his face in the waterhole. It was all over in a minute and he looked embarrassed by those tears but Pip didn't care. She smiled at him to show it.

'That's a creepy smile,' he said, so she punched him instead.

He placed his hand, palm up right near hers, sitting side by side, so she'd take it.

And she did.

'I'll keep it until she comes to get you,' said Pip.

THE PUB SMELLED OF WET AIR CONDITIONING and spilled beer. Men's sweat and men's cologne and Coca-Cola in a tiny tin that Matt bought for her as soon as she arrived. Pure sweetness in a tin. He bought it so her mother had to wait outside longer. Worry and sweetness in a tin. She was too scared of him to say no.

'Can I take the keys out to Mum?' Pip asked. Her mum was out there waiting beside his four-wheel drive, in the dark.

Matt pretended he couldn't hear. Raised his chin and tapped his ear. Shook his head. It was loud in there; the air conditioner *thrum, thrum, thrummed*. A giant thrumming artery, pulsing. It said: RUN-RUN-

RUN-RUN-RUN-RUN-RUN-RUN-RUN. The laughter of men rose and fell, rose and fell.

'One more for the road,' said Matt, and his words were slurred.

The barmaid leaned forwards and said something. Something about Pip not being allowed inside. *You know the rules, Matt,* or something like that. Her mouth was moving without sound, a green stone glinted at her throat.

Pip sipped on her Coca-Cola. She worried for her mother out in the carpark waiting. Worried for the drive home. Worried for Little Fella in the wardrobe. Maybe he'd wake up and fly, because now he really *could* fly.

'You don't smile much do ya?' said Matt's bar mate, a man with so many freckles that it took her breath away.

'Takes after her mum,' said Matt.

They laughed at that.

'Wait out at the entrance,' slurred Matt, leaning down near her ear. 'But where I can see you or I'll forget to come out.'

His words were heavy like boulders and loud in her ears and she recoiled from the smell of him.

'Stupid as,' she heard him say, as she walked away. 'Stupid like her mother.'

It started as soon as he was outside. He wouldn't give her mum the keys. He pretended he was going to drive and she refused to get in the car with him in the driver's seat.

'Come on, we'll walk,' her mum said to Pip.

'Lighten up,' he said, shaking his head. 'You're never up for a laugh nowadays, Mel.'

He got out of the car and stumbled, threw the keys at her, which she dropped.

Pip picked them up from the ground.

He sat in the back.

'You two sourpusses sit in the front,' he said, and then he laughed like it was the funniest thing he'd ever said.

'You're not actually that funny, Matt,' said Mum, driving carefully out of the pub carpark.

He snorted at that.

At home, Pip rushed to her bedroom and opened her wardrobe. Little Fella still slept, his little round belly rising and falling. She sat on the edge of the bed, trying to get her heart right. Her breathing right. She could hear her mum offering Matt his dinner. He didn't want his dinner.

'I'm having a beer first, sweetie,' he said. Then, 'Don't just stand there, all right. I'm. Having. A. Beer. What part of that don't you understand?'

She could smell her mother's fear, drifting down the hallway, when she'd thought she couldn't do that fear-smelling thing anymore.

Her mother's fear smelled terrible.

Like the dirty water in a vase of wilted flowers, weeks old.

She looked at Little Fella and let out one small sob. Her skin tightened, released, tightened, released. Both her thighs now and the backs of her knees.

What will happen to me? she wondered. Maybe it would tighten one time and not release. Maybe it would tighten and tighten and tighten and squeeze out her insides through the top of her head like toothpaste from a tube.

She put her head in her hands on her bed and sobbed again.

In Townsville they'd never feel like this. Not ever. In Townsville they'd dive into the clear sea and wash away the stain of him.

She heard him out in the kitchen, fumbling in the fridge, stood up and closed her bedroom door and turned out the light. She picked Little Fella up out of the wardrobe and carried him to her bed. 'I don't want you to go.'

He woke and rolled onto his back and she tickled his tummy.

She bit a piece of the apple that Laura had stolen from her fruit bowl and let Little Fella sniff it. She didn't know what he'd make of it. He was on all fours immediately, crunching and dribbling apple juice. It made her laugh despite everything. His lava lamp eyes glowed in the dark.

Matt didn't go off.

She heard the microwave eventually.

Her mother creeping quietly to bed.

She heard beer top after beer top ping against the sink.

There was no fight.

The house was quiet.

The street was quiet. The stars and moon strung up in a glittering swathe lit up her bedroom.

'How will I know when you can go?' she asked Little Fella in the dark.

Little Fella crunched on the last mouthful of apple.

It was soon. She answered that question herself. Little Fella wouldn't be coming with them to Townsville. She knew it, the way waves know to crash on a shore and trees know to reach for the sun. She was surprised that she didn't feel devastated by that. She felt sad, a deep tender sadness like a bruise, but knowing it made her feel stronger too.

'What will happen when you're gone?'

She whispered that too. And in reply he butted her hand, to be patted, to be scratched behind his tiny dragon ear. Along the rubbery nubs of horns.

She thought of Laura and Archie across the streets; they'd be lying in their own beds thinking of Little Fella too. They were all changed. They could never go back to what they were. She smiled in bed, curling around Little Fella. She couldn't wait to see them again, her friends, in the morning.

AT THE END OF THE SECOND YEAR OF MIKA, the river came down. First there was heat. Unbearable heat. It was worse than the normal bitumen melting heat. It was strange, crackling, ominous heat. People stayed inside. They closed their venetian blinds. The swampy air conditioners hummed and chattered street after street and mirages shimmered at the end of every road.

Then there was faraway thunder from the edge of the blue sky.

'Where's that even coming from?' said Mika, at the waterhole.

'Big storm coming,' said Pip, dipping her feet down through the scalding top layer of the waterhole, into the cool.

Mika raised his face to the blue sky, closed his eyes.

'I can't even remember rain,' he said.

He wasn't pale anymore. Mrs Jarvinen had filled out the flesh on Mika's bones and the sun had turned his pale skin brown. Pip had changed too. At school she no longer shapeshifted, she didn't sit at the edges so much.

'Bet you this is all gone by tomorrow,' said Pip.

'Gone?!'

'When the river comes down.'

'Huh?'

'The river will run, Mum said it, it's been raining up in the gulf too.'

'What!?'

'Bet you a million dollars this place will be filled with water by tomorrow. Meet you here as soon as the sun comes up.'

That night a curlew called, a haunting lament, hour after hour until a storm ripped out of the north and tore into town. It lashed the streets and peeled away some shed roofs and brought rain in torrents, deafening, drumming rain, for hours and hours and just before dawn, the burrowing frogs awoke and began to sing. Pip lay in her bed, listening to them, thinking of Mika.

In the morning the sky was scrubbed clean and the earth, eucalypt-breathed, smelled relieved. They heard the deep whisper of the river long before they saw it, streets away.

'What is that?' asked Mika.

'You'll see,' said Pip.

Other people had arrived early too. People had driven there and walked there and ridden their bikes. Archie was there with his brothers. Laura Denning was there with her family, wearing matching gumboots, because that was the type of family they were.

And the river was there, the wide brown river, its back rolling, rippling, carrying everything it could grab to take with it: trees, broken eskies, wine cask bladders, a saddle, fence posts, gallon drums. It had swallowed the crossing whole. It slapped up against the silver box gums. The small crowd cheered when a shopping trolley floated by, jammed itself against the submerged crossing, then flipped and sped along.

Pip and Mika left the crowd and rushed along the bank, picking their way through long grass, and dipping heads under the bent branches of snappy gums.

'Watch for snakes,' said Pip.

The river rushed close by their feet. One slip and they'd be in trouble.

'Hey!' shouted someone. 'You kids be careful.'

It took a while because the big wide river had stolen their landmarks. Eventually, they found the approximate spot where the waterhole should be. Nothing but river rushing, rushing, rushing on.

'The bunyip's really not going to like that,' said Mika, shaking his head.

'Maybe the bunyip likes having the water freshened up a bit,' Pip giggled.

'Hope it's still there when the flood's gone,' he said.

'The bunyip?'

'No, our waterhole.'

Our waterhole.

'It will be,' said Pip.

IN THE NIGHT, PIP COULD SMELL MATT. HE WAS
sour like milk gone off in the sun. He smelled of
dirt, sweat, unbrushed teeth. She could smell him all
the way from her bedroom to the living room where
he stood. Little Fella stirred beside her.

She could smell Matt's confusion too because he
was drunk. Stumbling.

She willed him to fall down and sleep.

'Fall down and sleep,' she said quietly, as though she
had such powers.

And she heard the crash of him hitting the sofa.

What if he could sleep for one hundred years
like in *Sleeping Beauty*? Only *he* would be Sleeping

Ugly. He could lie there and everyone could go about their business around him. Her mum could go to yoga without him laughing at her. She could buy the food she wanted to buy and she'd eat so much sushi that she couldn't move. She could take the credit cards out of his pockets that she helped pay off and buy herself the maxi dresses she looked at online. She'd enrol to study at university. It wouldn't be a curse. It would be a curse in reverse. And maybe if someone could save him with a kiss then they could, that'd be fine, and maybe the kiss would make him better or someone else altogether. Or if no one was available for the kiss then that would be fine too. He could go on sleeping. They'd pack their bags and close the door without even saying goodbye. They'd simply leave him sleeping there.

She tried to sniff for his fear but smelled nothing. His fear was hidden away too deep. She fed Little Fella by the light of the stars and felt desperate for the day.

When dawn came, she tiptoed out to the kitchen and packed her supplies. She knew Little Fella would need to go to the toilet soon, so she figured she might as well be prepared. The kitchen was filled with pale morning light. She took two apples. More Weet-Bix.

She froze when she heard Matt groan and shift on the sofa in the next room. He didn't wake. She took two water bottles. The clock on the windowsill said 4:45 in shining blood-red letters.

'Ouch,' she said as her skin tightened. She saw her left arm shimmer momentarily from the corner of her eye. A wave of quivering light, gone just as quickly. She gasped as she held her fingers up to her face, examined them. They were glowing, ever so slightly.

She closed her eyes, opened them again to see if it was real.

The glow was still there, although fading.

She breathed out slowly, watching the light disappear, until they were ordinary fingers again.

She brushed her teeth as quietly as she could, dressed in yesterday's clothes, glanced at the remnants of the braid in her hair and decided to keep it. She stared at herself in the wardrobe mirror. On the outside she was the same girl as five days ago yet she looked braver now. Felt braver. That new braveness gave her a small thrill, a ripple of something in her heart, and her skin creaked.

So brave, said Mika faintly in her ear and she gasped. The relief made her feel limp.

I thought you were gone.

There was sudden movement behind her in her reflection. Little Fella had launched from the bed and, flapping frantically, landed on her shoulder. He rattled and then hissed happily.

Still here, said Mika except he sounded the farthest that he'd ever been.

I'm glad, said Pip and she wanted to tell him about the light in her hand but even before she could begin, she sensed he'd vanished again. She placed Little Fella in her backpack. Scooped Mika's stones from her drawer and placed them in her pocket. She peered into her mother's room and offered a silent apology.

Dawn was steadily filling the house and she knew she had to leave. The dragon was heavy in her backpack and restless too. She walked quickly and silently down the hallway. One glance at Matt's sleeping profile where he lay sprawled on the sofa.

'Goodbye,' she said softly.

She took the back steps, careful to not let the screen door bang, breathed in the new day, all the rattlepods, dirt and dry yellow grass. All the sulphur fumes and blue sky. There were still some stars clinging to the end of night. She felt excited suddenly. She lifted Little Fella carefully from the backpack and he did his business in her mother's rose garden.

'Quickly,' she said.

Because she thought she'd heard footsteps and she'd frozen again. She didn't want to be so scared. It wasn't fair to be so scared. She scooped him up even though he wanted to play in the dirt, and noticed there were new buds all over the rosebushes. She let out a long sigh at that.

'Wow,' she said to Little Fella as she placed him in the backpack. 'You've got really good poo.'

His eyes were shining brightly as she zipped him up.

She rode down the street, her tyres on bitumen the only sound. The stars winking out in the sky and the day's moon rising. Everyone still sleeping. Everyone still dreaming. Not one of them aware that the girl who saved a dragon was riding past.

IN THE CAVE SHE FED HIM APPLE, HIS NEW
favourite food. She wondered if there were apples
where he came from. He watched her thinking,
crunched and dribbled, sat on his haunches, twitched
his little dark wings. Maybe when she was older, she'd
tell her mother. She'd say, 'Mum, so this thing happened
to me when I was ten . . .'

What would it be like to look back on?

'Will you forget about me?' she asked Little Fella.

That thought made her sad, so she stood up and
offered her forearm and he sprang upwards easily from
his sturdy hind legs and landed there, his tail wrapped
around her wrist.

'They'll be here soon,' she said and they both gazed out at the day, which was growing bright and shimmery with heat.

Laura came first. She leaped down from the drop-off in her pink ballet leotard with its sheer pink skirt. No ballet shoes, instead a pair of flip-flops decorated with purple flowers. Her hair was in a high doughnut-shaped bun. And she looked like she'd been crying, her eyes puffy and her nose red.

'What happened?' asked Pip, worried Laura might have betrayed them. It must have been written all over her face, because Laura shook her head.

'I didn't tell anyone,' said Laura. 'I've run away from home.'

'Run away?'

'From home.'

'From home?'

'Stop repeating everything I say.' Laura put her head in her hands and sat in the dirt and really started to cry. Little Fella climbed into her lap so she had to stop being so dramatic and scratch his horn nubs.

Laura wiped her eyes and nose with the back of her hand.

'It'll be okay,' said Pip. 'You know it will be. You'll go home.'

'Mum said, "don't you dare go" and I said, "I'm going forever".'

'Why'd you even say that?'

'Because she was being so mean,' said Laura, fresh tears falling down her cheeks.

'Oh,' said Pip. And she could almost imagine another conversation about the right types of friends. 'Don't worry. Don't be sad.'

'Has he had breakfast?' asked Laura, wiping at her tears again.

'Apple!' said Pip.

'Apple?'

'I know! He loves it.'

'You're so clever eating apple,' said Laura to Little Fella and she scratched his ears. He seemed very pleased. 'Why isn't Archie here? I thought he was coming early?'

'I know,' said Pip. 'It's weird. Should we be worried?'

'No, he's safe, one hundred per cent,' said Laura.

'Any songs?' asked Pip.

'No. I'm not a Dragon Singer anymore,' Laura said and it seemed like a fresh storm of tears was about to commence.

'But you were,' said Pip. 'And that's what counts.'

Archie arrived not long after. 'Sup,' he said after he leaped down onto the ledge. He looked at Laura, who had finished crying again and was rubbing at her eyes. Little Fella was asleep in the crook of her left arm.

'Nothing,' said Laura.

Even though she'd run away from home and was no longer a Dragon Singer and she didn't want the dragon to leave. That was the main reason she was crying. It was so obvious. *She should just come out and say it*, Pip thought. *And then it would be done.*

'My mum made me do one hundred jobs,' said Archie. 'I was like, *Mum*, I've got important places to be!'

'He eats apple,' said Laura, ignoring him.

'That's wild,' said Archie and he shook his head. 'Who ever heard of an apple-eating dragon?'

They were all quiet.

'So,' Archie said, sitting down with his back against the day.

'So,' said Pip.

'So,' said Laura sadly and she started to cry again.

They sat in a circle and waited for him to wake.

Little Fella eventually opened his sleepy eyes and they all sat up from where they lay in a circle around him. *There couldn't ever have been a more loved creature*, Pip thought. Laura, the Dragon Singer, scratched him under the chin. Archie, the Dragon Trainer, checked the sky for danger. Pip shuffled forwards on her bottom, to prepare his Weet-Bix. She still didn't know her role though she knew it was more important than mushing up cereal. She stared at her heavy aching hand and it seemed like a perfectly normal hand. There was no way to explain that to Archie or Laura. There was no way to explain the glowing, shimmering light she'd seen.

'You've really got to be careful up here,' she said to Archie. 'There's sure to be hawks in the morning.'

'I know, I know,' said Archie.

'And maybe he should let his belly settle,' said Laura, as Little Fella slurped the last from the bowl.

'Look at him, he's ready,' said Archie. It was true. He was trotting towards Archie already, a determined glint in his eyes.

'Jumpandfly,' said Archie, holding out his forearm and their gazes fused. Training had begun.

Little Fella leaped and Pip felt the wind of his newly strong wings as he passed. He landed on Archie's forearm, raised his chin, hissed, rattled and then let out a screech. It was a small screech but a screech all the same.

'That's a new one,' said Pip.

'I think it means he's ready to fly big,' said Archie.

Pip bit her lip. She wondered if her arm would shine again when he flew. The two seemed to be connected.

'It's all clear out there,' said Laura.

'You ready?' said Archie and he threw his glance out of the cave and back to his forearm. 'Flybig.'

Little Fella leaped again from Archie's arm. He shot out with great force, maybe two metres, well over the edge of the cliff, then hesitated. He flapped frantically, then powerfully, until he caught some unseen current in the air, hovered, and turned in a graceful arc back to Archie's arms.

They all exhaled at the same time.

'Good boy,' said Laura.

Pip glanced at her hand and saw that nothing had happened. She was confused. She didn't understand any of it. There should be rules to magic. Yet even as she thought that she remembered Mika's words.

Some things you can't think.

Little Fella screeched again as though agreeing with those silent words. He raised his little head and screeched at the blue sky, and it was true, it sounded like the screech of readiness.

THAT LAST DAY IN THE CAVE THEY TALKED
about Little Fella and how they saved him. 'You
saved him first,' said Laura.

'I needed you to sing,' said Pip. 'Remember my
singing? It was getting me nowhere. You sung his
wings together.'

'You had already kind of half-mended them,' said
Laura.

Laura, who was always right, was changed. She sat
there, a runaway, in a dirty pink leotard.

'And I taught him to fly,' said Archie, and raised his
arms, shaking them in a champion's salute.

'I'm pretty good, hey?' he said, when they didn't

encourage him. 'You know an expert when you see one, don't you Little Fella?'

It was on the tip of Pip's tongue to tell them about the dragon scratch, her tight skin, the deepness of the hole in her hand, the light. Where to begin?

Tell them, said Mika, close to her ear.

She drew a spiral slowly in the red dirt.

'Remember how I had that bandage on my hand?' she started, opening out her palm.

Both Archie and Laura nodded.

'Well that was a claw scratch from Little Fella.' She hesitated. 'An accident. Anyway. My hand has been really heavy ever since and it aches a lot, like something is in it.'

An opening.

'Something like?' said Archie and Pip saw him shiver.

'I don't know.' Pip stared at the ground, made a circle with her finger in the dirt. She didn't mention the light. She couldn't. 'It's not a bad thing. I mean, it's just that you taught him how to fly, and you mended his wings Laura and I kind of know my thing has to do with my hand. And with my . . .'

She tapped her palm against her heart, lightly, in case saying the word would set off that rushing, swelling feeling. She didn't know how to explain it to them. She shouldn't have said anything. Laura was scooting across the cave floor and taking her hand between her own. She examined it carefully, felt its temperature with the back of her hand.

'See,' said Pip. A normal un-glowing, un-shimmering hand.

'But it must be something if you feel it,' said Laura. 'I mean, remember when I had the song and I was trying to stop it? I could feel it, inside.'

Pip saw her flush at the memory.

'It must be something,' repeated Laura softly. 'It has to be.'

Laura provided no solution but Pip felt better for having told them. She felt better for having Laura hold her hand. For having Laura tell her it must be something without trying to say what the something might be.

Some things you can't think, Mika had said.

You've got to let them be. Feel them maybe, Pip added silently in her head.

Archie, lying on his back, changed the subject.

'So, I've been wondering,' he said. 'Do you think Little Fella's mother will come for him?'

'She might,' said Laura, looking to Pip.

Pip could tell Laura hadn't thought of that before. Her worried expression had returned.

'She might,' agreed Pip.

'How big will she be?' asked Archie.

'Kind of big dog-sized,' said Laura.

'Elephant-sized, I reckon,' said Pip.

'I'm seeing B-double road train sized,' said Archie and he smiled at the image in his head. 'Now colour?'

'Definitely rainbow,' said Laura.

'Definitely black,' said Pip.

'I'm seeing blackish blue,' said Archie.

'That's not even a colour,' said Laura.

'Could be in the dragon world,' said Archie. 'And I'm going for fire-breathing.'

'Definitely fire-breathing,' agreed Pip.

'Rainbow-breathing,' said Laura.

'So, you've got a fluffy rainbow-farting Rottweiler.' Archie laughed.

'Shut up,' said Laura. 'I never said farting.'

Archie made a farting noise.

Little Fella made the friendly maraca rattle in return and they burst into laughter.

'She'll be friendly too,' said Laura, when they'd recovered themselves.

'Mothers are protective,' said Archie. 'She'll be lethal but we're safe because . . . you know.'

'My mum's super protective,' said Laura. 'Like . . . she knows every single thing I do.'

Her bottom lip quivered.

'That's a good thing,' said Pip.

'You reckon?' said Laura.

'I reckon.'

'Your mum is too,' said Laura. 'Isn't she?'

'Yeah,' said Pip, thinking. Her old mum had been. The mother that laughed and danced and called her Little Swan. The mother that bought the Piccadilly and the Double Delight.

'My mum would burn down the whole town if she was a dragon. She's got a temper when it comes to protecting us kids,' said Archie.

They were sitting in silence imagining all the possibilities of a fire-breathing mother for Little Fella when they heard a voice calling from above.

'**L**AURA!' SOMEONE WAS SHOUTING.
A man's voice.

'Laura!' A woman's voice this time.

Then another voice: 'Laura, where are you? Come out, sweetie!'

'Fudge-nuggets,' whispered Archie.

Laura's face was so shocked it might almost have been comical in any other situation. Any. Other. Situation.

'That's my mother!' she whispered. 'And my father . . . and my grandfather!'

'Quiet,' mouthed Pip, because there were footsteps right above and a small spray of pebbles skittered over the edge and dropped away below them.

'Can you see a cave?' Laura's mother said, clearly. 'I can't see a cave anywhere here.'

Laura's face had turned red and she had tears in her eyes again. Little Fella, startled by the voices, had crept backwards into her lap.

'Quiet,' mouthed Pip again, shaking her head, because Laura looked like she was going to lose it.

Archie put a finger up to his mouth.

'What about down under this ledge? If I could climb down, I might be able to see,' said Laura's father.

'Don't be ridiculous,' said Laura's mum. 'You'll break your neck. She wouldn't do anything that dangerous, surely.'

'You wouldn't know with the company she's keeping,' said her dad. 'Maybe we go back and start up from this side. We might be able to see from the base down there. Laura, can you hear us? You're not in trouble. We simply want you to come out!'

Laura shook her head, tears spilling.

The footsteps receded, and the sound of their voices calling her name did too.

'I have to go,' whispered Laura. 'I'll catch up to

them. If they come up this back way, they'll find us.'

Her hands hovered over Little Fella.

'You can't see the cave from the road,' whispered Pip. 'I know. And there's no way up. We checked it, Mika and I.'

'They might find a way, Pip. They're grown-ups. They'll think of something. You know it. And it's too risky. If they find him . . .'

She was up, wiping her eyes, smoothing down her ruined ballet skirt.

'You know,' she said to Pip, who had pressed two fists against her own eyes.

'I'm going to miss you, Little Fella,' said Laura, openly weeping now while she scooped him up. Little Fella nuzzled his head under her chin. 'I'm glad I had those songs for you. I'll never forget you.'

She handed him to Archie, looked at Pip, who wouldn't look at her, then climbed back up and over the edge. They heard her footfall and then a splattering of rocks rained over the ledge as she took off running. They heard her call out, 'Mum! Dad! Grandpa! Wait!'

*

At first, they stayed silent. Pip kept her eyes covered, straining to hear their voices and wondering if they'd return. Far away, they heard a car start up.

'We better go,' whispered Archie at last. 'I mean, they would have seen our bikes. They might come back.'

Pip shook her head.

Archie fed Little Fella some apple. He was itching to fly but Archie kept talking to him softly. 'Not now, little dude. Not yet.'

It was all a waiting game, was how Pip saw it. Her stomach rumbled and she ate the remains of Little Fella's apple. Laura was in her bedroom waiting to be scolded and Archie was waiting to lock eyes with Little Fella again and get him up into the sky, and across the streets Matt would be awake waiting for her mother to make a mistake and her mother was waiting to be free and Mrs Jarvinen was waiting for the day to end so she could sleep and not think of Mika, and the whole world was waiting for one thing or another. And there she was, Pip, waiting to return the dragon to where he came from.

'Why'd Laura say all that?' said Archie. 'Like she'd never see him again.'

'I dunno,' said Pip. 'Maybe she knew her parents were going to completely ground her.'

'I guess,' said Archie although he didn't sound convinced.

'Do you want to go to the creek? He could do some more flying there.'

'Yeah.'

They climbed back over the ledge and up and over the hill and their bikes were still laying where they dropped them except Laura's was gone.

Everything will be okay, said Mika.

'Come on,' she said to Archie. 'Race you there.'

THEY LAY ON THEIR BACKS, ON THE BANK,
while Little Fella scampered over them, snuffling
and nuzzling. Then, when he was ready, he flew three
more times, farther and farther in a great loop from
Archie's eyes and back again.

'Ouch,' said Pip, because this time when he flew
the tightening had returned. It was everywhere now:
her feet, her legs, along her thighs, her tummy, her
chest, both arms too. It was worse than ever before.

'What is it?' asked Archie. 'Your hand?'

Pip shook her head, waiting for the wave of
tightening to pass. The painful heaviness in her hand
pulsed.

'Watch,' she panted.

She held out her open palm and it shimmered for several seconds. White light shivered and twitched and then vanished.

Archie backed away on his bottom, his mouth open.

'Something's happening,' said Pip. 'I'm . . .'

'How'd you do that?' whispered Archie. He looked scared.

'It's not a bad thing, I know that,' said Pip. She didn't like the fear in his eyes.

'Are you sick?' he asked. 'Should we tell your mum?'

'No,' said Pip. 'Not yet. I think it's normal.'

Archie raised his eyebrows.

'Well, normal when you've found a dragon,' she said.

'You're freaking me out.' Archie smiled to cover up his nerves.

'It's gone again,' said Pip, showing her hand and he seemed to relax.

'Maybe it was just the sun?' said Archie softly.

The sun was starting its slide again, touching all the silver roofs and setting them ablaze with light.

Pip smiled at him. 'Maybe.'

'You know how I said you were wagging because of missing Mika?' Archie asked, serious now, not looking at her.

'Yeah?'

'But really you had a baby dragon,' he said.

'Yeah.'

He didn't say anything else. And there didn't seem to be any point to his questions, only there was. Pip knew there was. Words were useless. They were nothing but sounds connected to images. Some things were bigger than that.

'I miss him too,' said Archie at last and even that sounded small.

'I know,' said Pip, even smaller. Pains and heartaches made words seem like tiny scratches. 'Laura too. I didn't know that.'

'Yeah, she had to go to sick bay and everything. And she didn't come to school for days, like you.'

'True?'

He nodded, gazed at Little Fella.

'I better go home; my uncles are coming all the way from Boulia.'

'I better go too,' lied Pip.

'Maybe we should ride past Laura's and see what's up?' said Archie.

'How will she know we're there?'

'We could make the dragon screeching noise,' he suggested, a grin spreading across his face.

He demonstrated the noise and, sitting on Pip's knee, Little Fella screeched joyfully in return.

They rode past Laura's house, screeching like baby dragons. One pass, then again, until Mrs Denning came out and told them to stop it. 'Go on,' she shouted, 'off you go! Laura can't play today.'

Pip performed a lazy circle on her bike, in front of Laura's house.

'Should I get Mum to ring up for a play date?' she asked cheekily.

She knew she'd never see Laura's mum again.

Archie screeched like a dragon and from deep within Pip's backpack, sleepy Little Fella added his own. Pip saw movement at Laura's bedroom window; the venetian blinds lifted and there was Laura, smiling sadly.

'Close those blinds this instant!' shouted Mrs Denning.

Laura didn't. She raised her hand.

'Tell him I love him,' she cried out, waving. 'Tell him.'

'I will,' shouted Pip. 'I promise.'

And then as they rode away, because Mrs Denning was striding now, furiously, towards the front gate, Laura mouthed the words, 'Thank you.'

THE LAST ROCK MIKA GAVE HER WAS BLOOD-
red. It was a pebble, worn smooth by a millennia
of flooding rivers, like no other pebble in that area.
The river running had brought it there. 'Look,' he said,
digging it out from where it was wedged in amongst
plainer pebbles. 'It's like a drop of blood. You're my
blood sister.'

'Aren't we meant to cut ourselves for that?' said Pip,
accepting the rock on her palm.

Mika had been so glad that the waterhole returned.
He'd hollered and leaped from the bank, landing in the
ankle-deep river. He'd sprinted, spraying water behind
him, to the raised area where the waterhole sat and

peered into the sepia-coloured pool. It was the last day although they didn't know it then.

Pip wished she'd known it.

She would have said things that were much more important.

'Oh yeah, that's right, you faint with blood,' she said, teasing him.

She held the blood-red stone in her fist while he lay on his belly and traced his finger around and around in the new water.

'This place is special,' he said again. 'Can you feel it?'

'You always say that,' said Pip, to annoy him by not agreeing.

'You know it is,' he said, quieter, tracing the spiral. 'This place is magic. Do you believe in it?'

She wanted to say no but that wasn't telling the truth. They sat in silence and the first dark clouds cast a shadow across their waterhole.

'Say you do,' he said and he sounded sad.

'I do,' she said. 'Of course I do.'

'My mum rang,' he said, so quietly that Pip almost mightn't have heard it.

'What!' cried Pip. She jumped up, sat down again. 'Is she coming? Aren't you excited?!'

'Yeah,' he said. 'She's probably a couple of days away. She's picking me up.'

'Oh,' said Pip. That didn't seem possible. Of all the impossible things that Mika had told her, this was the most impossible. Headless headmasters and poltergeists and werewolves and towns swept away by molasses and spirit orbs and spells and portals to other realms and one hundred billion stars in one galaxy.

She's picking me up.

Her eyes stung and she pretended to examine the storm clouds for a long time.

'Did you know that the Milky Way has at least one hundred billion stars in it?' he said after a while, to help her. Somewhere there was the distant rumble of thunder. Another storm on its way. A week of storms. Up north flooded with an inland sea.

'Yes, you've told me one hundred billion times.' She was surprised at the anger in her voice. He just kept going, though.

'If you had the choice would you be cryogenically frozen and go to another star, Pip?' he said. She shook her head at him, at the randomness of the question.

'Can I get unfrozen again and come back to see my mum?'

'Maybe,' said Mika.

'Maybe?'

'Well, probably not. She'd probably have died thousands of years ago by the time you got back.'

Pip didn't think you should ask that sort of question. And she didn't like the idea of being frozen. And she didn't want him to go. On the spaceship. In the car with his mum. He couldn't go, just like that.

'Maybe you don't even need to be frozen,' he continued. 'Maybe the aliens have good technology so that we could travel at the speed of light or maybe they know how to go in a space–time wormhole so that you could come back before you left.'

Pip sighed.

'I hope you don't go on the spaceship,' she said to Mika. 'Unless you know that you can get back.'

'I'll check with the aliens before I decide,' he said and smiled at her.

She wished she'd said something better that last time. Something with meaning. The news that he was being picked up had shocked her though. It had stolen all her good words. There were storm clouds, a tower of them emerging from the north, and the air filled with a strange electricity. She said, 'See you tomorrow, right?' The tiny blood-red stone inside her fist, clenched tight.

More thunder, somewhere, far away.

'See you tomorrow, Pip.'

*P*IP TRIED TO LIE TO ARCHIE.

Yes, see you tomorrow.

Yes, we'll meet at the cave.

Yes, I think it'll be safe.

No, I think Laura won't be allowed out.

She was kind to him but Archie was smart. He knew something was different. She could see him remember the light that had shimmered over her hand and with that memory she watched the waves of goosebumps that rose on his arms.

'What's happening, Pip?' he said, at the end of their pretend plans for tomorrow. 'Something's happening, right? With your hand. With that light. With Little Fella.'

The day was growing shadows. The galahs were passing in great drifts across Gallipoli Park.

'It's okay, Archie,' she said. 'I promise it's okay.'

He kicked his blown-out sneaker against the bitumen but didn't argue. He dropped his bike with a clatter to the ground and walked five paces away, turned back. He was full with emotion yet he contained it, breathed it out.

'You know it,' said Pip and he nodded.

He unzipped the backpack, for one last peek.

'See you tomorrow, little dude,' he said, his voice breaking.

Then he rode away, without once looking back.

$\mathcal{S}$HE DIDN'T GO HOME. SHE NEEDED THE CAVE
again, she knew it, the way water winds towards
the sea or a seedling pushes up through dirt towards the
light. The cave, and when the time was right, the
waterhole.

But first she went to Erap Street, Little Fella sleeping
in her backpack.

She rode there slowly, as though she had all the time
in the world, performed lazy figure eights on her bike in
the middle of the empty road. And Ursa sat on the top
of Mrs Jarvinen's neat brick fence watching her.

'Hi,' Pip said eventually, when she had worked up
the courage. She dumped her bike on the footpath

and approached the cat yet already there were tears in her eyes. She wiped at them angrily. Ursa arched her back and stretched. She was large; no sign of that tiny dishevelled kitten, her coat sleek and snow white.

'I just wanted to say goodbye.' Pip patted her on the back and heard her purr.

In Townsville there'd be sunshine. There'd be a small house with ceiling fans and the smell of mosquito coils. She'd help her grandmother care for orphaned possums. Her mother would wear the dresses she loved and every night she'd tuck Pip into bed and call her Little Swan. She had tears on her cheeks now and her words were rushed. She knew she couldn't stay.

'And I'll never forget you. I'd take you but I think Mrs Jarvinen needs you more.'

Pip rested her forehead against Ursa's. 'Look after her,' she whispered.

Mrs Jarvinen's tiny car was in the driveway and Pip knew she'd be inside, sitting at her table, or maybe in front of the television, staring. Pip wouldn't go in, couldn't go in. She couldn't bear to see Mika's great-grandmother and her sadness. She wasn't brave enough yet for that.

Pip's legs ached this time as she rode back to the cave. Her stomach whined as she climbed the hill. Other children would be getting called inside. They'd be sitting down for dinner.

When they were back in the cave, she unzipped the backpack. 'Come on, Little Fella,' she said, because she knew it was the right thing to do. She'd wait there for a while, looking out over the land, all the hills turning pink with the sunset and the grasses glowing gold.

It was a good thing.

An important thing.

One of the most important things she'd ever do in her life although she knew, right then, that she'd do many. The dragon skin she'd grown had started to split. It had split at her wrists like a too-tight coat and it was cracking over her back. It wasn't an unpleasant feeling at all. It was a freeing feeling and she thought perhaps it must be how it felt to be a seed.

Little Fella lifted his head to the sunset.

For a while, time didn't move forwards in the cave.

It *swelled*. It moved sideways and backwards and forwards and in circles. She went over and over the story of the dragon and over and over his little body so that she would never forget him. Claws and the nubs of horns. The perfect new tufts of fur and healthy shimmer of his dark scales. His wings, newly strong. She didn't want to forget an inch of him. She didn't want to grow up and have him faded in her mind. This dragon that she'd always known.

She fed him one last time. Arrowroot for old time's sake. He leaped out into the sky and returned in a gentle arc to her forearm before the meal, as though testing his wings. A shiver of light played over her hand.

'Not yet,' she whispered to him. 'Not yet.'

He watched her with his golden eyes and she knew he understood.

'Are you still here?' she asked Mika, in their cave.

Yes, he said from far, far away.

*H*IS MOTHER HAD COME FOR HIM, THAT much she knew. She came in the white Holden Commodore, licence plate 966MOP, nearly two hundred and fifty thousand on the odometer. She came across the Nullarbor and turned inland up through the Never Never and when she hit the tablelands she drove through the storms. She had her foot on the pedal, because she really needed to see him. She arrived in the night and knocked at the bedroom door and his heart woke even before his mind and his feet, knowing it was her.

He probably said, 'All night, I felt it. I felt you were nearly here.'

Because that was a Mika kind of thing to say.

Mrs Jarvinen would have turned out the light on them, sleeping together in his little bed, with dawn already coming fast and the earth already turning towards their last day.

Maybe she said, 'Are you ready?'

'For what?'

'To go?'

'What? We can't just run off on Nan.'

Maybe she said, 'But we've got to go. I've got to keep moving. I don't want him to find us.'

'I've got to say goodbye to people, to Pip.'

'You have to pack your stuff.'

Maybe that's what happened. Maybe he said, 'I don't want to go.'

Maybe he wept over Ursa.

Maybe she said, 'Oh, I get it.'

Because all love comes with thorns.

And he would have regretted his words, and stood up to start packing everything into his little green backpack. His yellow torch, his Russian–English dictionary, his *Unexplained* magazines, the entire universe, his folded map of Australia with his wished-for dotted line.

But when Mika and his mother left early that last morning the earth had other plans for them. That's the way the earth is. It's always changing itself, rewriting its face. It showed Mika and his mother the sun except the creeks and the rivers were fat with brown water, bulging at the banks, gobbling up trees, crashing over bridges.

Perhaps Mrs Jarvinen said, 'Don't be silly, you can't go. All the crossings will be over for sure. Here, I'll get it on the radio so you can hear it for yourself.'

She wouldn't have wanted him to go. She'd grown fond of him. Mrs Jarvinen was thin and dry as a piece of old bark but she grew new shoots on kids.

Perhaps she said, 'Please don't take him. Leave him here with me where he's thriving.'

The bridges in town were still open. That would have given Mika's mum a false sense of safety. Perhaps she saw the way miners, on the way to the day shift, ploughed through the few centimetres of water as though it was nothing. It was a crossing out on the way to Cloncurry that tricked them.

White Holden Commodore number plate 966MOP.

Pip didn't like to think of it. She thought of it a lot.

The way that it happened, without knowing what really happened, because no one would say. They all just whispered it. That story was torn up into single words. *Pity. Shame. Wouldn't. Have. Known.*

Should. Have. Known. Better.

He spoke to her and he spoke to her and he spoke to her those first days. His voice was clear and close to her ear.

Don't be sad, Pip. Please don't be sad. Promise me you won't be sad. Remember the closest star is eighty thousand light years away Pip and one light year is nine point five trillion kilometres but still you can see its light, right? And what do you get if you cross a kangaroo with a sheep? A woolly jumper. And did you know that ghosts can fly? I mean, like, really fly, like ride the wind and it makes you laugh so loud. And you shouldn't blame my mum, Pip. She really didn't know. And what do you get if you cross an elephant with a kangaroo? Big holes all over the outback.

Don't be sad. Please.

Remember Sagittarius A swallows all light but it's not a bad thing. It's just a thing. It's just a black hole, like a river is a river filled up with rain and a tornado is a wind turning fast. Maybe we got across and maybe we went to live in Kalgoorlie. Magic happens, Pip. Promise you'll take your feet out at dusk because that's when the bunyip comes out.

And he spoke and he spoke and he spoke while she begged him, curled in her bed, frozen there, *Mika, Mika. Tell me it's not true.*

If she could have, she would have said more that last time, when there was the thunder and the storm in the distance and the whole day crouched as though it knew what was coming.

It would have been huge, what she would have said. Sky-huge. Galaxy-huge. Universe-huge. It would have stopped clouds in the sky. It would have stopped the earth from spinning for just a second, the force of it.

ALL THE WAY TO THE WATERHOLE, SHE
wondered if Little Fella would remember it,
but it was the waterhole that remembered *them*. That
whole place was waiting. The dry grass knew them
and the dark water too.

Pip sat down with Little Fella in her lap in the last
light. They only had minutes. She knew it. She slipped
her feet into the water.

The galahs settled down into the trees, they fell pink
and grey, and the day called the night. And day and
night would come to the place forever and the stones
would shift and the waterhole would dry and fill again
but they only had these few minutes. Only minutes.

Something was about to happen.

She took the stones from her pocket and gave them back. The piece of black meteor, the pink and gold quartz, the white dragon's egg, the blood-red stone. She dropped them one by one into the water and they disappeared. The skin along her left arm tensed, quivered.

She felt the splitting sensation yet where she looked there was nothing, nothing there splitting on her skin.

She felt Little Fella tense too, the shiver of his muscles beneath her fingers.

In her left hand, there was a sudden intense burning that snatched her breath away. Her heavy hand, her healing hand, grew bright and the pain was so sharp that she called out, she was sure of it.

A light.

A pure light poured from her hand, upwards.

And she knew, it was part of herself.

Little Fella's snout went up and the tufts bristled along his back at that light. There was an immenseness to the sky, to the day slipping away, to the coming night. But that light was larger. That light, right then, was infinite. She felt the tremble of his wings.

Something was about to happen.

Up he leaped and she felt the weight of his hind legs press down with force against her thighs. Up!

He flew into her light, which he gathered up around him in a fraction of a second, in the blink of an eye, in a single heartbeat. It folded in on him, it collapsed him into a pinprick of light that winked once,

as the last rays of the sun hit the creek

and shone that place alight.

Before the flood of dusk,

before night.

And he was gone.

THERE WERE NO LIGHTS ON AT HOME AND
Matt's car was parked in the drive. Pip opened
the front door quietly and her mother was seated in
her chair in the living room. The room smelled of
dirt and beside her were two buckets. One contained
Piccadilly. The other Double Delight. Her mother
sat in darkness yet even then, Pip could tell her eyes
were swollen from crying. She stood before her
mother, touched her face gently.

'Where is he?' Pip said.

'He went out,' whispered her mother. 'He took a
taxi but he took the car keys too.'

Pip's heart sank.

Only her mother unfolded her hand and showed a key.

'Mum and Dad said they'll drive to Hughenden to meet us,' her mother said quietly.

Pip dragged the suitcase from beneath her mother's bed and into it she flung her mother's clothes, then her own T-shirts and shorts on top. Her dragon skin creaked across her chest, split, she shed strips of it there in that room. Toothbrush. Hairbrush. She stared at her mother's phone lying beside the pillow.

Rose fertiliser. Common problems with roses. How to fix dying roses. Transplanting and transporting bare-rooted roses.

Domestic Abuse Hotline. Getting out safely.

It *ping*ed and she jumped. A message from Matt.

'Leave it there,' her mum said, standing at the door.

Pip left it on the bed. The message unopened.

Outside she placed the roses in the back of the car, the buds opening now and filling the night air with their perfume. She looked up at the blazing Milky Way.

Mika?

She knew he was gone, but she longed for one last word. Any word. And even though she was crying, she felt a strange bruised happiness, too.

Thank you, she said. Because that's what she was. Thankful. The suitcase that she heaved up into Matt's four-wheel drive seemed small, and everything they were, was too big for it. She was strong and brave and so was her mother too. She knew it.

One day she'd write to Laura and Archie; she could see it already in her mind. When they got to where they were going. Where the sea sparkled down at the end of the street and her mother studied by a window. She'd tell Laura and Archie what happened and maybe she'd meet them again one day, when they were older, and they'd sit together and remember Little Fella.

When she sat inside the car the dragon skin tore along her thighs. It creaked up and released along her chest. She felt like she could breathe for the first time in years.

'Drive, Mum, just drive,' she whispered as her mum put the four-wheel drive into reverse and backed slowly out onto the street. Her heart was swelling.

There was newness and goodness waiting for them.
'Don't look back.'

They drove through the dark streets, towards the outskirts of town and then the town was behind them, all the streets swallowed up by the hills and the mine disappeared behind the ranges and then there were only the stars ahead of them.

Acknowledgements

This novel began as one of several short stories for a collection of children's fantasy stories set in outback Australia. *Dragon Skin* was the only story that survived from the project, and in doing so it continued to outgrow its form, becoming the novel it is today. Those original stories were developed with the assistance of the Australian Government through the Australia Council for the Arts. I am so grateful to have received funding to research ideas and to travel to the town I grew up in, to walk those streets, explore the dry river and hills I climbed as a child.

Those readers who know Mount Isa will recognise the town, or parts of it. It's a strange and wonderful place, a long way from anywhere, the country of the Kalkatungu people. I apologise in advance for any inconsistencies between the town of my memories and the town of today. I chose to make *Dragon Skin* a modern story, or at least one set in the last decade, yet my mind kept throwing back to the town of my childhood in the 1970s. I fused these two together in many instances. In the end, all I hope is that the incredible harsh beauty of that place shines through.

As usual I'm indebted to the good people at Allen & Unwin, especially Anna McFarlane, for really helping me to make this story grow in so many ways and Nicola Santilli for her skilful editing. I'm grateful for the first reviewers, Katrina Nannestad, Edwina Wyatt, Bren MacDibble and Leanne Hall. Much thanks also to my agent Catherine Drayton who encouraged me to pursue these ideas from that very first rough story, and Dale Newman for her beyond perfect artwork. Her illustrations and cover are everything I hoped for and more.

Finally, if you are in a situation where you do not feel safe, if there is someone in your life who makes you feel bad, who hurts you, who makes you feel worthless or who tries to control you, you should talk about it with someone you trust. You should tell a friend, a teacher, or call the organisation below for help.

Childline
0800 1111 • www.childline.org.uk/

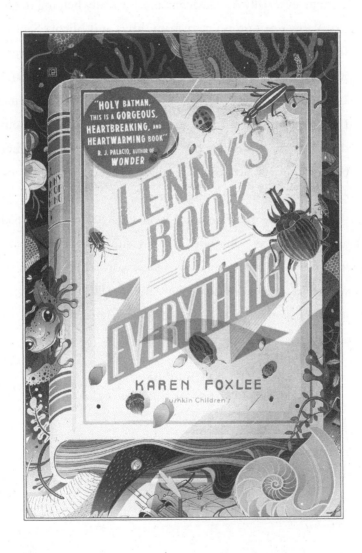

AVAILABLE AND COMING SOON
FROM PUSHKIN CHILDREN'S BOOKS

We created Pushkin Children's Books to share tales from different languages and cultures with younger readers, and to open the door to the wide, colourful worlds these stories offer.

From picture books and adventure stories to fairy tales and classics, and from fifty-year-old bestsellers to current huge successes abroad, the books on the Pushkin Children's list reflect the very best stories from around the world, for our most discerning readers of all: children.

THE MURDERER'S APE
SALLY JONES AND THE FALSE ROSE
THE LEGEND OF SALLY JONES

Jakob Wegelius

WHEN LIFE GIVES YOU MANGOES
IF YOU READ THIS

Kereen Getten

BOY 87
LOST
MELT
FAKE

Ele Fountain